CHEERLEADERS

#4

FEUDING

LISA NORBY

SCHOLASTIC INC.
New York Toronto London Auckland Sydney Tokyo

ISBN 0-590-33405-C

12 11 10 9 8 7 6 5 4 3 2 1   4   5 6 7 8 9/8 0/9

FEUDING

CHEERLEADERS

Trying Out

Getting Even

Rumors

Feuding

All the Way

Splitting

CHAPTER

1

"*D*EE-fense! *DEE*-fense!"

Mary Ellen Kirkwood jabbed the air with her fist in time to the pounding rhythm of the cheer. The temperature in the overheated gym was above ninety degrees and her feet and ankles ached from doing cheer routines on the concrete apron that ran along the sidelines of the Muskeagtown High School's basketball floor.

In spite of her discomfort, she looked like the ideal cheerleader: blonde and blue-eyed with a perfect figure.

True, she hadn't particularly noticed the heat as long as it looked like a sure win for Tarenton High. Now with the Tarenton Wolves' star center, Hank Vreewright, out with an injury, the Wolves' game plan was starting to fall apart. And Mary Ellen felt as if she might disintegrate along with it.

As the cheer ended, Mary Ellen turned to the

members of the squad standing nearby. Her face still glued into a smile that could be seen all the way up to the top row of the bleachers, she wailed through her clenched teeth, "What a disaster!"

Olivia Evans and Nancy Goldstein regarded her calmly. Sometimes Mary Ellen wondered how much those two really knew about sports anyway. Fine cheerleaders they were!

The whole of Tarenton had been holding its breath, hoping that Hank's famous glass knee, the veteran of several operations last year, would last through the season. Unfortunately, those hopes had been in vain. Hank was out of commission for the foreseeable future. And within minutes of his departure, the Muskeagtown Maulers had narrowed Tarenton's lead to a scant five points. Jimmy Hilbert was put in in Hank Vreewright's place. But Jimmy wasn't Hank.

"Who *is* this Jimmy Hilbert, anyway?" Mary Ellen screeched in frustration. "I mean, I've seen him around school. But I didn't even know he *played* basketball. Where did he come from, all of a sudden?"

"Well *I* knew he played," Olivia said evenly.

"So did I." Nancy, at least, couldn't resist grinning openly at this unexpected chance to top Mary Ellen in sports savvy. "He's pretty good, they say. He can't help it that he's had to sit on the bench all season while Hank hogged the spotlight."

Mary Ellen was stunned. Only a few weeks ago, she'd had to explain to Nancy what a full court press was. Since when had *she* become such

2

an expert? And what was all this about Hank Vreewright hogging the spotlight? At six-foot-ten, he was Tarenton's only hope for state All-American.

Mary Ellen shot a supplicating glance in Angie Poletti's direction, looking for help in defending Hank's reputation. But Angie, the squad's most enthusiastic and knowledgeable basketball fan, was momentarily distracted. Mary Ellen noticed that she was trying to catch the eye of a darkly handsome young man with a mustache who happened to be sitting about twenty rows back in the section reserved for visiting Tarenton adults. Suddenly the young man noticed Angie looking his way and grinned, flashing a set of movie-star perfect teeth.

Angie's reaction to the greeting was cut short by Pres Tilford and Walt Manners, the male contingent of the squad, who were calling for the girls to join them in the "Growl, Wolves, Growl" cheer. Mary Ellen ran down the sidelines a few steps ahead of Angie and the others, relieved that someone still seemed to have some enthusiasm left.

Part of her mind, however, was occupied with the scene she had just witnessed. For all her wholesome image, Angie had dated older guys before. In fact, she was still semiofficially going out with Marc Filanno, a Tarenton grad who was now away at the state university. This new mystery man of Angie's was definitely older than Marc by a few years. Mary Ellen guessed that he might even be in his thirties. If so, no wonder

Angie hadn't mentioned him to any of her friends from school!

Out on the court, the last minute substitute, Jimmy Hilbert, was more than living up to Nancy's review of his abilities. Snatching the ball in midair, he robbed the Muskeagtown center of a sure basket and bounded downcourt toward the Tarenton basket. There, ignoring the signals of his teammates, who were calling for passes in their direction, he lobbed in a shot from outside and watched with obvious satisfaction as it circled the rim three times before dropping in for a score.

Pres hoisted Nancy onto his shoulders so that she could be seen in the far reaches of the bleachers, and Walt followed suit with Olivia. Once again, this time more hopefully, the squad launched into the growl cheer.

> "We've got the bite!
> We can't be beat!
> Come on, Wolves,
> Let's bare our teeth!"

"Grrr . . . rrr" began the response from the visiting Tarenton cheering section, the low growl gradually building into a menacing crescendo and ending in a full-voiced roar.

Mary Ellen grinned to herself at the response, recalling that when she had first proposed adding this new verse to the cheer, Olivia had objected. "But beat and teeth don't *rhyme* . . ." she'd said plaintively.

It had taken a ruling from coach Ardith Engborg to override Olivia's objection. "I don't think the English faculty is grading cheers for literary merit," Ardith had said. "At least, so far, none of them has suggested it."

Tonight Olivia appeared to have set aside her problems with the bad rhyme. "Are we sharp?" she bellowed through the megaphone.

"*Yesss. . . !*" roared the Tarenton fans.

"Then let's do it again," Olivia commanded. "Come on!"

On the court, as if on cue, Jimmy Hilbert repeated his earlier maneuver, snatching the ball from the hands of one of the Maulers and bounding downcourt for another solo basket. Mary Ellen held her breath, sure that he had committed a foul, but apparently the referee had missed the beginning of Jimmy's move. The basket counted, lifting Tarenton to a comfortable seven-point lead.

"Not exactly what I'd call team play," Walt said dryly, referring to Jimmy's single-handed scores.

"Maybe not," Pres said. "You can't argue with success, though. I'm sure I never do."

Olivia had heard that little exchange between Walt and Pres, but she'd decided to keep her opinion to herself. Later, in the section of the girls' locker room that had been assigned to the visiting cheerleaders, she hurriedly claimed one of the few private shower cubicles for herself and began to undress.

She always felt a wave of relief when the away

game facilities turned out to offer her a chance to change out of sight of the other girls. She was the only girl on the squad who hated being seen nude. She had a small, compact body that made her a dazzling gymnast.

But comparing her own body to Angie's and Mary Ellen's well-endowed figures was enough to throw her into a depression for days, if she let it.

Olivia had another reason for not wanting to change in front of them. Her secret consisted of three vertical scars running up the center of her chest, reminders of the open heart surgery she had survived as a child. Plastic surgery had made the scars much less noticeable than they once were. Her mother kept telling her they could hardly be seen at all, but Olivia didn't believe it. She felt sure the scars were so disfiguring that her world would end if anyone discovered their existence.

Tonight, however, she was not about to let anything happen to bring out her feelings of inferiority. Olivia had promised herself just last Sunday that she was going to change her image. And so far, her plan was working out beyond her wildest dreams. Only yesterday she had accepted a date for next Saturday's school dance with Jimmy Hilbert. And now, after warming the bench for an entire season, Jimmy had suddenly emerged as the hero of tonight's game.

Olivia could hardly believe it. Even though she'd been on the crack Tarenton cheerleading squad for months now, she still felt like an impostor most of the time. Most of the rest of the squad had earned their places, not just through skill but by being among the best-looking and most popular students at school. Olivia, though a good athlete who could do amazing routines, was not in their league socially. She had told herself for months that she didn't mind. Popularity was not really important in the long run anyway. So all the advice columns in the magazines said, anyway. From the outsider's point of view it sure looked like fun, though. And for once, Olivia was determined to grab some of that fun for herself.

"Eat your heart out, Michael," Olivia muttered under her breath. Then she did her best to ignore the wave of pain that flowed through her at the thought of Michael Baines.

In her more reflective moments, Olivia felt that she and Michael belonged together. But so far, the relationship had been more headaches than it was worth. Michael was even more competitive than she was, if that was possible, and like her, he put in long hours to achieve perfection in sports, schoolwork — anything he set his mind to. As a result, he and Olivia did not see enough of each other to make her feel they were a real couple. And when they did manage to find time to spend together, more often than not their moments alone were ruined by some pointless misunderstanding.

No more! Olivia promised herself. From now on she was going to stick with guys who knew how to enjoy themselves.

7

Jimmy Hilbert and Olivia Evans. . . . Olivia rehearsed the combination of names in her head, as she toweled herself dry and struggled into her clothes in the tiny cubicle next to the shower. Tall, happy-go-lucky Jimmy and petite, high-strung Olivia. The rest of the world might consider the two of them an unlikely couple, but Olivia was well on her way to convincing herself that the match was destined for success.

Before heading for the parking lot, Olivia waited outside the boys' locker room to catch Jimmy alone to deliver congratulations in private. Then she headed outside to the yellow mini-bus that was waiting to take the Tarenton cheerleaders and their gear home.

As usual, the players' bus had completely loaded and pulled out of the parking lot ahead of them. Mary Ellen and Nancy straggled out to join the rest of the cheerleaders, looking surprised that once again their fussing over makeup had kept the others waiting.

For once, even Coach Engborg didn't show any sign of impatience. "Well, squad," she said contentedly as the driver got under way, "I'm very pleased. Not only did our team win, but tonight you looked like a team yourselves. I think we are finally transforming ourselves from a bunch of individualists into a true squad."

Mary Ellen, seated a few rows behind Ardith on the other side of the aisle, looked up in surprise. Only this evening she'd been feeling like she wanted to strangle Olivia. And she still had to fight down pangs of jealousy every time she looked at Nancy Goldstein, with her perfect little gold earrings and those fawn-colored calfskin boots. Fortunately, no one else on the squad seemed aware that Nancy spent more on a single pair of boots than Mary Ellen's mother earned in a week.

Mary Ellen decided that Ardith was basically right. Except for herself, the rest of the squad fit together. Mary Ellen was grateful that no one else was aware of the ringer in their midst.

Seated beside Mary Ellen, Angie Poletti was smiling and nodding in agreement with Ardith's little speech. Nancy and Olivia looked contented as well. And Walt, always a dynamo of energy, was already out of his seat, demonstrating his latest version of a Michael Jackson dance step. Ardith, usually a stickler for using seat belts, let him finish his routine before motioning him back into his seat.

Pres, from the row behind Mary Ellen and Angie, led the appreciative laughter that greeted Walt's performance.

Unknown to Mary Ellen, Pres had noticed her moodiness and found himself liking her better for it. Pres had always admired Mary Ellen's cool, blonde good looks. Physically, he and Mary Ellen were similar, his dark blond hair and blue eyes complementing hers. But he'd also assumed that they had nothing in common when it came to their personalities. Behind Mary Ellen's sweet face and baby-blue eyes, she was a bundle of ambition. Mary Ellen dreamed of leaving Tarenton behind on the day after high school graduation and going on to a successful career in the world of high fashion modeling. Her chances were good, too. Pres, for his part, wanted to leave Tarenton to *escape* success, not to find it.

Pres had been in sixth grade when he first came to realize that his family's house on the peninsula overlooking Narrow Brook Lake was known locally as the Tilford mansion. At first, he'd thought the name was a joke. By now he knew better. It wasn't just that the Tilfords lived in a fancy house and drove fancy cars. No one in Tarenton was likely to forget that the Tilford family had founded Tarenton Fabricators, the only major industry in town.

Pres did his best to forget how different his family was, but last night he'd been reminded once again that the Tilfords were hardly your average Tarenton residents. His dad had insisted that he hurry home from squad practice to make an appearance at a dinner party. On his way up the walk, he had caught a glimpse of his parents, waiting for their guests in the living room. Both of them were wearing evening clothes. And Martha the maid, who usually wore slacks and an old sweater to work in, had changed into a long-sleeved gray uniform. Pres couldn't help thinking that the gathering looked like something from a *Masterpiece Theater* production. Not what most Tarenton kids came home to — not by a long shot.

Pres had gone up the back staircase to change, and when he came back down into the foyer, his parents still didn't realize that he'd arrived home.

"I've put up with it long enough," he heard his mother saying as he neared the living room door.

"I wasn't aware that you'd been suffering, Felicia. It seems to me that you have a very pleasant life." Mr. Tilford was using the aggrieved tone of voice that he usually reserved for father-son arguments.

Sensing that something was up, Pres had stopped short in his tracks and eavesdropped.

"I'm not without resources," his mother had said then. "I can always live with Hildy until I get a job."

Bit by bit, Pres figured out that his parents were discussing a separation. He'd been bowled over. Not that he'd ever thought of his parents' marriage as especially ideal. But he'd always assumed that Tilfords didn't get divorces. Those kinds of things happened in *other* families. Not to people like them.

Twenty-four hours later, Pres was still in a mild state of shock. If his parents did split up, there was no way he could stay in Tarenton with his father. Without his mother to referee their arguments, he and his father would drive each other nuts in two weeks. On the other hand, he couldn't exactly imagine where he'd fit in Aunt Hildy's city apartment in St. Paul. And for that matter, his mom hadn't sounded as if she had any intention of inviting him along.

Pres enjoyed being the one in the family who kept things stirred up. But he didn't much care for being a passive pawn in his parents' quarrels.

His name hadn't even been mentioned in the conversation he'd overheard.

Pres drummed his fingers uneasily on the armrest of his seat and stared out at the snowflakes whipping past the bus window. He wondered when the other members of the squad would stop rehashing tonight's game long enough to notice that the weather had suddenly turned very nasty.

CHAPTER

"Hold on!" Ardith's warning rang out just in time. The bus, which had been in the middle of a winding downhill curve, suddenly slipped sideways into a skid. While the driver fought to regain control, the passengers stared ahead of them in open-mouthed helplessness. A car, that minutes earlier had been approaching them in the oncoming lane, hit another patch of ice and lurched directly into their path. By a combination of skill and sheer luck, their driver managed to guide the bus over toward the shoulder, missing the car's rear fender with only inches to spare.

"That was close," Pres said, whistling softly in relief. From his seat in the back row he'd had a good view of the face of the driver in the other car. He'd heard of people's eyes popping out in fear, but until now he'd always thought it was just a figure of speech.

"I thought I was going to lose that hot dog that I stuffed myself with at halftime," Angie said with a laugh.

"Don't be so gross," Nancy gasped. "And don't mention food. Not *now*. Please." The blood had drained from her face, leaving her normally tawny complexion a sickly shade of yellow.

"Please God, just let us get home safely," Mary Ellen prayed, addressing the general direction of the bus ceiling. "We'll be good from now on."

"Some of us have been good all along," Pres shot back, regaining his cool. "We don't have to bargain now."

"That's true," Olivia piped up. "But I don't see how you get the nerve to include yourself in that group, Preston Tilford the Third."

Mary Ellen heard a voice giggling loudly. It was her own. She had to give Olivia credit for her coolness. For someone who seemed like such a baby at times, Olivia always had nerves of steel when everyone else panicked.

"Cool it, everyone," Walt said. "We ought to be thanking the driver for saving our necks."

The bus driver, who so far hadn't said a word, acknowledged the round of applause led by Walt with a barely perceptible shrug. "We were lucky that time," he said. "I'm getting off at the next exit to wait for the salt spreaders. The road's a sheet of ice and I can't see a damn thing, what with the sleet coming straight at me."

"Well, that certainly instills confidence," Nancy

14

whispered in a voice that came out louder than she'd meant it to.

"Nonsense, Nancy," said Coach Engborg, reaching back to give Nancy a comforting pat on the shoulder. "You just haven't lived in the north country long enough. Winter storms are a way of life."

"That's why Ardith has the garage order a spare set of fenders for her car every October," Walt added. "Just to be prepared." Walt knew that the coach didn't always appreciate teasing, but he couldn't resist. Ardith Engborg was not really a bad driver, but her house had the steepest driveway in Tarenton and her fender-benders were legendary.

"What would you know about the problems of winter drivers?" Mrs. Engborg shot back, only half jokingly. "*You* have four-wheel drive, I notice."

Walt grinned in mock apology and headed for the front of the bus, to act as lookout for the driver. The others stared out the windows in silence. They reached the next highway exit and the bus picked its way around the cars stalled on the upgrade around the exit ramp, and began to proceed slowly but steadily toward a neon sign that blinked fitfully in the distance.

"Whadya know!" Walt crowed from his spot up front. "Great minds think alike."

Peering up ahead, the others saw that the Tarenton team bus had obviously just arrived in the same diner parking lot.

The manager had to unlock the door of the diner to admit the passengers from both buses. "You're welcome to wait out the storm here," he said, "but I can't serve you anything except sodas and coffee. I sent my help home early to avoid the bad roads."

"That will be just fine," Ardith agreed quickly. "We don't want to put you to any trouble."

The answering groan of disappointment from the players suggested that the sentiment wasn't unanimous.

"Personally, I could eat a horse," one of the guys said. "I always get this starved feeling after we win. But never mind. I'll starve quietly."

The diner's manager studied the size of the boy who had made this speech, and began to reconsider his terms. No doubt he was thinking of the check a six-foot-four teenager could run up in the course of satisfying a major hunger. "Okay," he relented, "I'll open the grill. But I could use an extra pair of hands helping me. There'll be all you can eat free for the first volunteer."

"I'm your man!" Jimmy Hilbert bounded over the counter before anyone else could answer.

As the others distributed themselves around the various booths and tables, Walt and one of the team managers began to organize the orders. Within minutes they had served cold drinks, hot chocolate, and coffee all around, and the first hamburgers were beginning to emerge from the kitchen.

For forty minutes or so, an impromptu party spirit reigned. Then the food was finished, and everyone began to look restless. Finally, the driver of the team bus got up from his corner table and paid his check. "Looks like the visibility has improved," he said. "I think we can make it now with no problems."

"I'm staying put," the cheerleaders' driver announced. "One near miss a night is enough. We wait here until the road crews come through."

As the players prepared to reboard their bus, Nancy Goldstein looked at Ardith pleadingly. "Why can't we go with the team?" she suggested. "There would be plenty of room if we moved some of their equipment into our bus. Then our driver could bring the gear home whenever he's ready to start."

Ardith shook her head. "I don't think so. Our driver has gotten us here safely so far. I trust his judgment. We'll wait it out."

Half an hour later, the highway was still unplowed and even Walt Manners was beginning to show signs of impatience to get home. Angie, finishing off her third cup of hot chocolate, surveyed her companions and wondered if now would be a good time to break the news she'd been saving for tomorrow's practice. At this rate, the practice would be canceled anyway.

Angie tapped her spoon against the side of her empty cup. "You're probably all wondering why I brought you here," she joked. "But I've got some great news. Did any of you notice that cute guy who was sitting in the reserved seat visitors' section?"

"I saw him wave at you," Mary Ellen said.

"Wellll . . ." Angie announced, "he's my cousin. Thomas Gaetano!"

Mary Ellen looked disappointed, the others merely confused.

"Another deep, dark secret from Angie Poletti's sinful past," Walt said sarcastically. "You've got a million of them, Ange. But so what?"

Angie was undeterred. She never had been good at wording things, and had long ago learned to accept her role as the target of self-appointed wits like Walt.

"That part wasn't the news," she said, ignoring Walt's comment. "The news is, Tom's a great guy. And starting Monday he'll be teaching at Tarenton High! He's taking over Mrs. LeMoyne's English classes!"

"This *is* news, even to me," Ardith said. "What's happened to Gloria LeMoyne?"

"Oh, her husband's company decided to transfer him to the Philippines," Angie explained. "She knew for months that it might be coming, but couldn't say anything until the official decision came through."

"No wonder she always seemed distracted," Nancy said. "She never gave homework assignments."

"That," added Walt, "is why I'm not exactly ecstatic about Angie's secret. LeMoyne also gave me an A last semester. Finally, Tarenton gets a teacher who recognizes my natural flair and brilliance, and they have to ship her out of the country."

18

"An A!" Nancy howled in outrage. "But you never do any work. Mrs. LeMoyne just favors guys, I guess. Especially ones whose parents have a daily TV show."

Mary Ellen was feeling vaguely guilty that she'd been so quick to think that Angie was dating a man in his thirties on the sly, and she wanted to make amends. "Angie's cousin is a real dreamboat," she assured the rest of the group. "He looks nice, too. I wouldn't mind being in his class."

"Don't let that statement get back to Patrick's ears," Walt teased.

"Patrick!" Mary Ellen looked cross. "What does he have to do with it?"

"Everyone knows you and Pat are always lusting after each other," Walt said innocently.

"Patrick is a jerk!" Mary Ellen snapped. "And you can all tell him I said so for all I care."

If she hadn't felt so tired, Mary Ellen might have reacted less strongly. It annoyed her, though, that her real feelings for Patrick were common knowledge around school. She certainly hadn't mentioned them to anyone, so it had to be Patrick who'd been discussing her. That was part of the problem with him. Every time she let him kiss her, which she wanted to do constantly, he acted as if she was practically ready to get engaged.

Mary Ellen wasn't ready for a serious involvement with Patrick Henley. For one thing, he wasn't in the league she wanted to play in. For another, she found him all too attractive in spite of his deficiencies. She could well imagine that if

19

she ever did give in and decide to become Patrick's girl, she'd be hooked for life. Then what would become of her dream of going off to New York in search of fame and fortune?

"Pres here is more my style," Mary Ellen added flirtatiously. "Tall, blond, and rich. He just hasn't figured out yet that we're right for each other."

Nancy Goldstein couldn't help smiling in admiration of Mary Ellen's nerve. Mary Ellen was so beautiful that she was confident that she could get away with saying just about anything. If there were any objections, she'd easily managed to pass off her remarks as so much kidding around.

A combination of tiredness and the exhilaration of tonight's events was beginning to wear away Nancy's own natural reserve. She'd been impressed by Ardith's speech on the bus, and the squad's being all together like this. Sharing a minor emergency only increased her feeling that Ardith had been right — a real team spirit was growing. These kids weren't just fellow cheerleaders, they were her friends.

"I have a confession to make, too," Nancy heard herself blurt out. "I'm in love."

The others looked at her in astonishment. Obviously, she'd sounded more serious than she'd intended.

"I didn't really mean *in love*," Nancy corrected herself grinning. "Just carrying a heavy yen."

"You're worse at giving news than I am," Angie said. "You can't stop there. Tell us who."

"Never mind," Nancy said, retreating. She was sure now that she'd made a mistake to speak up.

It wasn't even true. She wasn't in love. Her boy-friend Alex had gone home to England just weeks ago. She'd only said what she did because she'd been feeling flattered and happy that another guy had asked her out so soon, and because she'd wanted to feel more a part of the group.

"Come on, Nance. You can't cop out that easily. Now that you've gone this far, you've got to tell us the guy's name," Walt demanded.

Nancy felt trapped. "Okay. Okay. Who was the surprise savior of tonight's game?"

"Jimmy Hilbert?" Angie, Walt, and Mary Ellen asked in chorus.

"Does he know?" Olivia asked in astonishment. "I mean, have you gone out with him?"

"Of course," Nancy said. "I went out with him just two days ago."

Two days ago! Olivia couldn't believe it. That was the same day Jimmy had called to invite her to the dance! She'd known Jimmy had a reputation for playing the field, but until now she'd managed to convince herself that his interest in her was different. Irrationally, she focused her jealous anger on Nancy. "One date is *certainly* undying love," she snapped. "Just remember to invite me to your wedding."

"What about you, Olivia?" Walt challenged. "As long as we're playing true confessions, what about you and Michael?"

Alone in the group, Walt Manners seemed oblivious to the fact that not everyone was enjoying the rap session as much as he was. Walt wasn't cruel, but he loved gossip and loved keeping

21

things stirred up. To him, it was a game.

Olivia had no desire to talk about Michael, though. Thinking fast, she decided to say something that would deflect the question. "Forget me, guys," she lied. "My only secret is that my love life is nonexistent. A big zero."

"That's funny," Walt said, not unkindly. "I was sure that you and Michael were a case of true love." Then he gave an exaggerated shrug. "What's wrong with the youth of today, anyway?" he asked in mock agony. "What happened to the good old days when true love lasted forever?"

Pres's hand slammed down onto the formica table top so hard that the sugar server flew up into the air and went flying off into Angie's lap. "I've had just about enough of you!" he yelled at Walt.

Walt looked bewildered. "What did I do?" he asked the group in general.

"For starters," Pres answered, "I notice that for a guy who's eager to hear everybody else's personal business, you never tell us anything about your private affairs."

"Honestly," Walt protested with a grin, "I haven't had any private affairs in *weeks*. If I do, you'll be the first to know."

But Pres was in no mood for humor. "In that case, you've got no right to stick your nose into other people's business. So put a lid on it."

Pres pushed his chair away from the table and stood up. His face was flushed with anger.

Angie had gone to school with Pres since the elementary grades and couldn't remember ever seeing him lose his cool this way. "Are you all right, Pres?" she asked.

"Do I look all right?" Pres groused. "It's just that I've had it with this dumb talk about romance. True love is a farce. The whole world is filled with people busy looking out for number one. The sooner you all wake up and realize that, the better off you'll be."

Having said his piece, Pres turned his back on the group and stormed out of the diner to wait in the unheated mini-bus.

Ardith, who had been on the far side of the room chatting with the bus driver, saw Pres's dramatic departure and approached the table. "What's going on here?"

"Who knows?" Mary Ellen answered on behalf of everyone. "We're just as confused as you are."

Ardith sighed. That's what she got for opening her big mouth to make a speech on friendship and togetherness. When would she ever learn?

CHAPTER 3

"Did you notice those cute little dimples that pop out every time he smiles?" one of the freshman girls asked.

"Did I ever!" her friend exclaimed. "And what about his teeth? They're gorgeous. He's definitely the handsomest teacher Tarenton High ever had. Maybe the handsomest guy in the world, period."

The two freshmen went giggling out of the girls' bathroom, leaving Vanessa Barlow to stew in her own curiosity. "I can't imagine who they're talking about," she said slowly. "Certainly not Mr. McGoughey. Not unless standards have changed since I was a freshman."

Cindy Hartman interrupted her application of mascara to give Vanessa a sideways glance. Was it possible that she knew something about school business that Vanessa didn't? "They're probably

24

talking about the new English teacher, the one who replaced Mrs. LeMoyne."

"Oh. Him." Vanessa recovered in time to pretend to know what Cindy was talking about. Silently, she berated her father for not bothering to keep her informed of goings-on at school. What was the point of being the daughter of Tarenton's superintendent of schools if you were the last to know about important developments, like the arrival of a new teacher in midyear?

Cindy put away her mascara wand and studied her face critically in the mirror. She couldn't decide whether Vanessa was putting her on or not. "Then you know about Gaetano?" she pressed.

"Sure. I just forgot." Vanessa threw back her head and started brushing her hair vigorously.

"Then you know who's cousin he is?" Cindy went on.

Vanessa stared at Cindy.

To describe Cindy as Vanessa's friend would be too strong a word. Vanessa Barlow didn't have friends. She had sidekicks. It was understood, by Vanessa at least, that anyone who associated with her had to be ready and willing to play a supporting role in the enthralling drama of Vanessa Barlow's life and times — enthralling to Vanessa, at least. Cindy had been her number one sidekick for several weeks now, ever since she whipped up some great food for Vanessa's last party and let Vanessa take most of the credit. But Cindy's term appeared to be quickly running out. So far she'd been abjectly loyal in public, but in private she'd begun to challenge Vanessa's bossy ways.

This time around, Vanessa decided to give Cindy a second chance. "Of course I know who's cousin he is," she huffed. "But I bet you don't. So prove it . . . you tell *me*."

Cindy smirked, Vanessa's trick being so obvious. "Angie Poletti's. Can you imagine plain, potato-faced Angie having a cousin who looks like that?" Cindy knew she wasn't being fair. Angie, though no great beauty, was hardly a potato face. In fact, she had so much vitality, so much healthy exuberance, that she was almost beautiful. She was a cheerleader who loved every minute of every routine. Cindy couldn't resist the opportunity to swing back into Vanessa's favor, though.

"So what else have you heard?" Vanessa had now dropped all pretense and was eagerly pumping Cindy for information.

"Angie thinks her cousin is the greatest thing since the invention of sliced bread, naturally. But I hear he's very strict. He gave his first period class *days* of homework to do, and this is just his first day. I bet he'll be a tough grader, too. I heard that the other English teachers were upset because Mrs. LeMoyne gave so many A's last semester. She was a real softy, you know. She just couldn't stand to give a low grade to any kid she liked."

This was news to Vanessa, who'd received a B-minus. It also infuriated her that Cindy knew so much more faculty gossip than she did. Silently, Vanessa promised to take the matter up with her father that very day.

"I suppose we'll find out for ourselves, when fifth period rolls around." Cindy suppressed a giggle. "It will be interesting to see whether Walt Manners can wrap this new guy around his little finger the way he did LeMoyne. The only work he did all first semester was when he arranged for the class to visit his house while his folks were doing their TV show.

"It certainly will be interesting." Vanessa gave her hair ten more hard strokes with the brush. Then she studied the results in the mirror. She couldn't decide whether the effect was worth it or not, since her scalp tingled harshly.

By the time lunch period arrived, Vanessa had formulated her plan. Dragging the none too eager Cindy with her, she made sure that they left the cafeteria a few minutes early and arrived in Thomas Gaetano's classroom well ahead of the rest of the class.

"How do you do, Mr. Gaetano?" Vanessa proclaimed as she swooped down on the desk where the new teacher was reviewing his lesson plan one last time. "I want to be one of the first to welcome you to Tarenton High. I'm Vanessa Barlow and my father is Dr. Frederick Barlow, the superintendent of schools here in Tarenton."

Mr. Gaetano appeared to take the momentous news in stride. Turning toward Cindy, he managed to extract her name from her, and then politely note that he was looking forward to having both girls in his class.

"We certainly hope that you'll be giving us more work in writing," Vanessa said. "Of course, there are always a few students in any class who are lazy. But most of us feel that writing practice is very important. In preparation for college, I mean."

"That's good to hear," Tom Gaetano said, hiding a smile. "In fact, I intend to do just that. I feel that no matter how much reading you do, knowledge is wasted if you can't communicate your ideas in clear English prose."

"I couldn't agree more," Vanessa said. Tossing her long hair over her shoulder in a gesture that Vanessa hoped reeked of mature glamor and self-assurance, she headed back to her usual seat in the rear of the classroom.

As Cindy settled in across the aisle, Vanessa looked her way and confided in a stage whisper loud enough for Mr. Gaetano to hear, "What did I tell you? He's *very* nice, no matter what Walt Manners says."

Cindy thought at first that Vanessa had gone too far, but a glance at Mr. Gaetano's face made her wonder. It wasn't easy being a new teacher, especially when you had to come in during the middle of the year, replacing someone who had made life all too pleasant for her students. Cindy felt sure that no matter how hard Gaetano tried to forget Vanessa's remark, he'd be driving himself crazy wondering just what Walt had been saying about him.

By the time Walt Manners arrived in class, he

already had one strike against him. Only he didn't know it.

Walt took his seat near the door, wearing his usual all-purpose cocky grin and listened as Mr. Gaetano announced his plans for the class.

"One new project I want to introduce starting right now," Tom Gaetano explained, "is a daily journal. *What* you write is not important, as long as you fill at least one notebook page a day. You will be graded on clarity of expression. And, naturally, on grammar and spelling. That goes without saying."

Walt felt his stomach do an automatic flip-flop. Just what he didn't need! So far, he'd managed to get through Tarenton High without revealing to anyone the extent of his problems with spelling and grammar. Most teachers gave multiple choice tests and his mom made a habit of practically rewriting his typed papers. Since Gaetano wanted on-the-spot writing, Walt wasn't sure how he could get around this particular assignment. He frowned.

"Is something wrong, Mr. Manners?"

Walt swallowed hard. "Yes. I mean, no. I was just wondering if it would be all right to type our journals instead of writing them by hand."

"No go. I realize that handwriting is becoming a lost art," Mr. Gaetano said, "but you'll be doing this journal in the classroom. I'm setting aside the first fifteen minutes of every class. The reason for that is that I want you all to develop fluency. I want to see your first attempts."

What Walt saw was disaster staring him right in the face. He'd never manage to pass English with this guy, much less get the mark he needed to stay on the cheerleading squad.

Unfortunately, the worst was yet to come. The journal writing period was starting that very day. "Remember, you don't have to write your deepest personal feelings, although that would be fine. Any topic is acceptable," Mr. Gaetano explained, as he announced the start of the session.

All around Walt, students bent over their fresh, unmarked notebooks. Some started almost immediately and wrote at a furious pace. Others stared at the blank page and then began making a few tentative scrawls with their ball-points.

Walt watched the activity around him intently, dreading the moment when he would be the only one in class who had yet to put a word down on paper. He felt frozen with fear and, as often happened when he got nervous, his grin kept getting broader and broader.

"I'm glad you're finding this so amusing, Mr. Manners."

Walt looked up and saw Tom Gaetano standing beside his desk. He didn't know what to say. Maybe he could save himself with humor. "Yeah. Ha-ha. It's the funniest thing, but my mind just went totally blank."

"Oh, come on, Mr. Manners. I'm sure you must have some opinions — about teachers, for example. Just put them down."

What's happening? Walt wondered numbly. First Pres blows his stack for no reason, and now this new teacher seems determined to ruin his life. What had he done to deserve all this trouble?

While Walt continued to study the ceiling helplessly, in the back of the classroom Vanessa Barlow was polishing off her third paragraph on the importance of communication. She felt very satisfied with what she had accomplished so far.

Vanessa wouldn't have been quite so pleased with her day's work if she could have seen what took place in the Tilford home late that afternoon. Pres and Kerry Elliot were seated in the Tilford library, snuggling on the oversized leather couch in front of a roaring fire.

"I think fireplaces are just dreamy," Kerry said happily, as she rested her head on Pres's shoulder. "Imagine having this to come home to."

"I never enjoyed it much until now," Pres said.

And it was true, too, even though Pres couldn't quite believe that he was feeling this way about little Kerry Elliot.

During the last two years, Pres had dated scores of girls, mostly the more glamorous types Tarenton had to offer. It hadn't bothered him very much that none of his romances had ever seemed to last very long. Life was easier that way, especially considering the girls he always seemed to fall for.

Pres still often found himself fantasizing about Vanessa Barlow's lush mane of dark hair and curvaceous figure. Admittedly, however, the nonphysical side of their dating hadn't been too satisfactory. How could it be, when any man, even one who wanted her, would have had to admit that Vanessa had the morals of a rattlesnake. Although she'd never used her venom on him, it was no fun watching her scheme.

Mary Ellen had been another mistake. Her blonde good looks were so much his own type that they seemed made for each other. But Mary Ellen never had figured out what kind of person he was inside, and she really wasn't interested. Pres was fairly sure that if she ever did psyche him out, she would be very disappointed. She wanted someone who would fulfill her fantasy of a man for her.

Neither of these lost chances had bothered him too much. There were plenty of other good looking girls in the world. Even in Tarenton. But the last girl he ever figured he'd find himself interested in was Kerry. Kerry Elliot, with her plump figure and flyaway, curly brown hair and way of wearing clothes that showed just how little she cared about style. What Kerry had was a sweetness, a vulnerability that touched Pres.

When he first realized he'd fallen for Kerry, he was sure he'd never get anywhere with her. She was dating Andrew Poletti at the time and only saw Pres as a distant, inaccessible, though desirable, upperclassman. Then Kerry had discovered the extent of her attraction to Pres. He could still remember the first time they kissed, how excited and nervous he'd felt all at one time. How soft and yielding she had been. After that, Kerry had decided to break up with Andrew.

But though Kerry was bewitched by Pres, she also was worried.

"If I could stop caring about Andrew so fast, and fall in love with you," Kerry explained, "then I probably wasn't ready to be dating just one person in the first place. I think I need time before I let myself get serious about anyone else."

That sounded logical, except that from Pres's point of view the decision to get serious was history. It had been made before he'd had time to even think about what it meant.

Pres kissed Kerry, gently, sweetly. He wanted her, but he also wanted to protect her from his strong attraction toward her. She was so young, so inexperienced that he kept his own feelings under control. He was not aware of the fact that Kerry, for all her outward softness, knew exactly how far she was willing to go with Pres.

Pres leaned down and kissed the top of Kerry's curly head. Tarenton's number one ladies' man was turning into a real softy. And at times like these, he didn't even mind.

"Why, look who's here!"

Pres felt the tension shoot up his spine. From the tone of his mother's voice he could tell that she'd been indulging in afternoon cocktails and was at least halfway to being drunk.

Until a few months ago, he'd never known his mother to drink during the day. But lately she had been doing it more often, and with every time her behavior became more strange. First she'd acted just depressed. The last few times, she'd been hostile.

"Hi, Mom." Pres disengaged himself from Kerry and stood up. His mother entered the room wearing a floor-length hostess gown of purple velvet. It was obvious she hadn't gotten dressed yet that day.

"Sit down, I don't want to disturb you," his mother said, plopping herself into one of the leather armchairs that faced the couch.

"You're not disturbing us," Pres insisted.

Mrs. Tilford waved her long magenta fingernails in a 'never you mind' gesture. "That's a lie. But I don't care. All Tilford men are liars." She fixed her gaze on Kerry as if noticing her for the first time. "You'll learn that soon enough, young lady."

"Uh, Mom, this is Kerry Elliot. I don't think you've met her before," Pres said, doing his best to change the direction of the conversation.

"Hello, my dear. A pleasure." Mrs. Tilford's gracious tone evaporated quickly as she turned back to Pres. "I don't suppose you know where your father is."

"No, I don't."

"I'm sure he's working late again," Mrs. Tilford said to no one in particular. "Busy, busy, busy, you know."

There was a pause while everyone tried to think of what to say next.

"You have a lovely home, Mrs. Tilford," Kerry said in a timid voice. "I love this room."

"It is lovely, isn't it?" Mrs. Tilford looked around vaguely, as if noticing the room for the first time. Then she giggled maliciously. "All of my son's little floozies just love it."

"*Mother!*" Pres begged.

He would like to have said a lot more, but he knew getting into an argument would just do more damage. The look of pain on Kerry's face made him want to protect her at all costs. And the best way to do that would be to get her away from his mother as soon as possible.

Fortunately, Mrs. Tilford made that easy. As if realizing that her barb had hit the wrong target, she got up and swept out of the room, leaving Pres to undo the damage.

"My mother's been upset lately," Pres explained hurriedly. "Don't take anything she says seriously. She just isn't herself."

"It's okay," Kerry said, not very convincingly, in a quivering voice. "I just want to go home now. Get me out of here, Pres."

"I will, Kerry. Just don't be upset."

On the drive home they were both silent.

Pres wished there were some way he could erase his mother's words from Kerry's memory, but he couldn't think of a way. Why, of all the girls who might have witnessed that particular scene, did Kerry have to be the one? Pres knew that Kerry already had trouble believing that his interest in her was sincere. She couldn't shake the suspicion that he was just looking for an easy conquest. He'd worked hard to get Kerry to trust him, and now his mother had undone his efforts in one minute.

"Please don't be upset, Kerry," he said again, as he dropped her off in her own driveway. "Promise me you won't."

Kerry smiled back, but she looked anything but calm. "I'd better go inside," she said. "I can't talk now, Pres. I'll speak to you later. Just let me be alone for a while."

When Pres got back home, his mother had retreated into her bedroom. A "Do Not Disturb" sign, taken from one of the hotels where she and his father had stayed on one of their trips to Chicago, hung on the doorknob. That evening, Pres and his father ate dinner alone, served by the cook. His mother never appeared downstairs.

CHAPTER

Mary Ellen leaped out of the passenger seat of Patrick Henley's truck and led the way into Burger Benny's, hoping that no one had noticed her and Patrick driving up.

Now that there was snow and ice on the ground, Mary Ellen's plan of bicycling home from practice had gone from impractical to physically impossible. Most nights, she took the public bus from school after practice ended, and met her mother in the downtown office where she worked as a clerk. Then they both caught a ride home with the co-worker who usually drove Mom. This system took an extra forty minutes or so, but Mary Ellen found it too humiliating and embarrassing to ask for a ride, when so many of the other kids in school had cars of their own. This afternoon, when Patrick Henley offered her a lift home in his garbage collection truck, she had felt almost grateful. That just showed how desperate she was.

Inside Benny's, Patrick ordered diet sodas for both of them and got around to saying what was on his mind.

"So what's this about me being a jerk?" he asked.

Mary Ellen stared at him, feeling her face redden. There was no point in denying she had said it. Patrick was no fool, and people who lied only made him more determined to get at the truth. "Who told you that?" she asked.

"I have my sources," he said coolly.

For some reason, Mary Ellen immediately thought of Olivia. She'd seemed in a strange mood the other night at the diner. But why would she go out of her way to tell Patrick about Mary Ellen's comment? Maybe she's jealous of anyone who has a boyfriend who doesn't fade away, Mary Ellen speculated. Now that Michael is so involved with running, maybe she wants to see the rest of us suffer, too.

Of course, it didn't have to be Olivia. It could have been Nancy, or Walt, or even Angie, who made no secret of her disapproval of Mary Ellen's opinion that a boy with a part-time job slinging garbage was not good enough for her.

Patrick watched Mary Ellen's confusion with amusement. In fact, his source had been the bus driver, who also happened to work part-time for Henley Trash. It never occurred to most people that bus drivers had ears. But this one did, and he'd wasted no time in informing Patrick what

38

Mary Ellen had said about him. Actually, he'd called her the stuck-up blonde, but Patrick had no doubt who he'd meant.

Unable to avoid the issue, Mary Ellen decided to try logic. "I didn't mean that you were a jerk," she began. "It's just that you get me all confused by coming on so strong. I'm not sure I want to be anyone's special girl right now, and you're always in such a rush to get serious."

Patrick thought this over. He'd always taken it for granted that Mary Ellen was the kind of girl who expected to be swept off her feet. Maybe he'd been wrong. "Okay," he said agreeably, "what do you want?"

Mary Ellen hadn't expected cooperation, and she hadn't bothered to think ahead that far. "I've told you before. We could see each other once in a while. On a friendly basis. But sort of low profile, you know."

Patrick lifted his palms upward in a gesture that said, "anything you want."

"Great!" Mary Ellen said, but secretly she was disappointed that Patrick hadn't pushed for something more serious. And exactly what did seeing each other "on a friendly basis" mean? The feelings she had for Patrick were not just friendly. They came from need and physical yearning.

Before she got out of his truck when he brought her home, Patrick took Mary Ellen in his arms and kissed her, lingeringly, slowly. When he pulled back, he grinned and said, "Just a friendly kiss."

Mary Ellen leaned toward him and he kissed her again, making her wish she had never said anything discouraging to him.

When she went into her house, her younger sister Gemma was seated in front of the TV. "Mary Ellen! Did you get a ride home?" she asked excitedly. "Who with? Was it Patrick?"

Mary Ellen dumped her coat and books in the nearest chair and made a face. "I'm afraid so. Patrick again."

"So why aren't you happy?" Gemma asked. "I think Patrick is awfully cute. And he's crazy about you. He even worries about you. I saw him on Saturday and he wanted to know if you got home safely from the game."

When Mary Ellen didn't answer immediately, Gemma assumed a knowing expression. "I get it," she said. "Patrick likes you. But you like Pres . . . and his Porsche."

"Gemma!" Mary Ellen couldn't believe that her own loyal sister would say such a thing.

"Oh, I don't blame you," Gemma said, turning her attention back to the old *Barnaby Jones* re-run. "What's wrong with preferring a Porsche to a smelly old truck?"

Mary Ellen strode into the kitchen and started throwing together the preparations for the family dinner. Sometimes she wished Gemma wasn't quite so smart. What was wrong with wanting to improve yourself, and thinking seriously about the future? When she put it that way, Mary Ellen was convinced her ambition was justifiable. But

Gemma's offhanded comments reduced everything to the crassest level possible.

Mary Ellen surveyed the ingredients for the
night's meal: a head of iceberg lettuce, leftovers
from last night's meatloaf, a can of generic
peaches with a black and white label. Was there
something wrong with her, because she didn't
want to settle for a lifetime of coming home after
work to meals like this one?

Vigorously tearing into the lettuce, Mary Ellen
started to feel a bit better about herself. It wasn't
that she didn't truly like Pres. She did. So from
now on, she wasn't going to let herself feel the
slightest bit guilty about keeping Patrick Henley
at arm's length.

On the other side of town, Olivia was sitting in
the front seat of a very different vehicle from
Patrick Henley's garbage truck — Jimmy Hilbert's spanking new, white Mustang. Instead of
the parking lot of Benny's, the two were parked
on a lovely scenic overlook above Narrow Brook
Lake, with a view of a group of ice fisherman's
huts below them and a ruddy winter sunset taking
shape on the far horizon. But while the setting
may have been a lot more glamorous, Olivia
Evans was feeling even more confused than Mary
Ellen had been.

All weekend long, Olivia had scarcely been
able to think about Jimmy Hilbert without feeling angry and hurt. Had he invited her to the
dance because Nancy had turned him down?

Olivia knew that Jimmy had a reputation as a happy-go-lucky type. But her pride rebelled at being anyone's second choice.

It had taken all Sunday afternoon for her to get up her nerve to call Jimmy and ask that they get together Monday after practice to talk. But when Jimmy heard her voice over the phone, he'd seemed completely oblivious to the possibility that she wasn't happy.

"Terrific!" he'd said right away, when she suggested a meeting. "You haven't had a chance to ride in my new car yet, have you? I'll pick you up at the gym, and we'll go for a little spin before I take you home."

Jimmy's confidence that Olivia only wanted to congratulate him for Friday night's game began to melt her resolution. So what if Jimmy dates other girls? she asked herself. You wanted a guy who'd be a lot of fun. Now, before you've even had an official date with him, you're acting possessive. Like a real wet blanket. You have no right to expect anything from him yet.

So Olivia didn't say anything about what she had been feeling on the drive out to the lake. When the car pulled onto the overlook, she decided that she'd better speak now or the chance would be gone forever. Timidly, she asked Jimmy whether it was true that he'd been out with Nancy Goldstein last Wednesday.

"Sure," Jimmy admitted.

He turned and stared into Olivia's eyes with practiced sincerity. "You aren't letting that worry you, are you? Nance and I are just good pals. Nothing serious. Now, my feelings about you are a different thing altogether."

As if to prove the truth of his words, Jimmy reached over and caught Olivia in his arms.

Olivia gasped with surprise, then responded mechanically to Jimmy's kiss. A small voice in the back of her head told her that she ought to be skeptical about Jimmy's explanation. It had been just a little bit too pat, as if he'd used that line before on a number of occasions.

For the time being, however, Olivia had a different problem. She wanted to enjoy making out with Jimmy. She'd been telling herself for days that when the moment came, she would. Now, however, she felt nothing. Nothing at all.

Olivia caught hold of Jimmy's left hand, which had been slowly but steadily moving from the back of her sweater.

"Come on. Don't be a spoilsport, Livvy," Jimmy pleaded.

Olivia pushed him away and sat as upright as possible in her seat. The word *spoilsport* ruined any chance she might have had of getting interested. It made her suspect, uncomfortably, that Jimmy regarded what they were doing as just another game, like basketball — a chance for him to score.

"I just don't think we know each other well enough, Jimmy." Olivia said.

"So? I was trying to get to know you better."

Olivia stared out her window. "You know what I mean."

"Yeah, I know." Jimmy reached for the ignition key and started the motor. "I just can't figure you out," he said. "First you're jealous because you think I might have a thing going with Nancy. Then, when I show that I'm really interested in you, you turn into an instant icicle. How can a guy win?"

Olivia couldn't think of an answer to that one, so she rode in silence the rest of the way around the lake. At least part of what Jimmy said couldn't be argued with. She didn't know *what* she wanted.

By the time they reached Olivia's street, Jimmy's good spirits seemed to have recovered. "Tell you what," he said, "why don't we go to a movie tomorrow night?"

"On a Tuesday?" Olivia usually spent Tuesdays studying for her Wednesday biology quiz.

"Sure. Live dangerously for once," Jimmy laughed. "There's a movie at Cinema Mile that I've been wanting to see and tomorrow's the last night it's playing. *Vartan the Viking*."

Sword and sorcery epics weren't normally Olivia's favorites, to say the least. But there was no way she could say so, and have any hope left of shedding her ice princess image. Thinking fast, Olivia remembered that her mother would be out tomorrow night, attending a fundraising meeting for the Heart Fund drive.

"Why not?" she told Jimmy. "As long as I get home at a reasonable time, there's no problem."

During the next twenty-four hours, Olivia changed her mind a hundred times. Not about

44

the movie. She was sure about that. But what would she do when Jimmy, inevitably, suggested going home by way of the scenic lake drive? If he stopped at the overlook again, would she be more encouraging than she'd been on Monday night? Or would she play icicle for a second time?

Olivia knew that other girls went through the same mental debates. But she was convinced that her case was unique. Others might have doubts about specific guys. Or about the wisdom of getting physically involved too soon. Or about going too far. Olivia knew, though, that other girls *enjoyed* kissing. She'd heard Angie talk about her dates with Marc, and about how tough it was sometimes for her to say no. And the other girls in the group had all seemed to know what Angie was talking about.

Olivia had never felt that way. Well, maybe just a little bit with Michael. But he was so elusive that she hadn't had much of an opportunity to sort out her emotions on that score.

With Jimmy, she'd been sure it would be different. He was handsome, suave, and confident. But at close range he left her cold. She was sure it must be her own fault. Nancy certainly wouldn't feel that way.

After school on Tuesday, Olivia dressed with special care. She wore corduroy slacks, a cotton shirt, and a blazer — nothing too dressy. But she had carefully put on eyeliner to accentuate her wide-set brown eyes, and she wore her best pair of earrings: tiny garnet posts that had been a birthday gift from her favorite aunt. Fortunately,

45

her mother wasn't around to insist that she bundle up in three layers of sweaters under her winter coat. Olivia had told her mother that she was going to the movies, and received her grudging permission. But if Mrs. Evans had been home to supervise her preparations, Olivia was sure she'd have ended up looking as if she were headed for an assault on the South Pole instead of a simple trip to the movies.

Jimmy seemed to appreciate the results of her efforts. "You look great," he said as they headed for the line that had formed inside the theater lobby.

"Thanks," Olivia said apologetically. "It's nothing special. I'm too short to wear sophisticated clothes, unlike some of the girls on the squad."

Olivia wished she could bite off her tongue. Why had she said that? Actually, she loved chic clothes. She just didn't have any. And everyone knew that the only sophisticated dresser on the squad was Nancy Goldstein.

Jimmy hadn't missed the reference. "Yeah," he agreed, "Nancy's a very sexy girl. Uninhibited, if you know what I mean."

Olivia felt herself tighten. She clamped her jaw firmly shut. Did that mean what she thought it did? Was it true? She'd certainly never thought of Nancy in that way. But then, what did she know about that whole side of life? For all she knew, every single one of her acquaintances at Tarenton was miles ahead of her when it came to sex. She was the freak.

"Speaking of sophisticated dressers," Jimmy commented as they edged their way toward the waiting ticket taker.

Vanessa Barlow, with her friend Cindy in tow, had just entered the theater. She was wearing a short, fun-fur jacket, with a high neck and a fringe of tan, black, and white fur tassels along the bottom edge. Underneath, her legs were encased in skintight black pants of a shiny, satin-like fabric. High heels — which must have been tricky to walk in across the snow-encrusted parking lot — finished off the outfit.

"I think calling that sophisticated is an understatement," Olivia said mildly.

"What I can't figure out," Jimmy said, "is why a girl gets herself up like that and then never appears in public without at least one tag-along chaperone."

Olivia was about to answer, when they reached the head of the line and entered the dimly lit theater. Jimmy firmly steered her toward the tiny balcony set above the entrance door. "We'll be cozy back here," he grinned, draping his arm heavily around her shoulders.

Olivia squirmed. Naively, she hadn't thought about the possibility that Jimmy intended to concentrate on something other than watching the exploits of *Vartan the Viking*. She wasn't ready for this. Not yet. Not *here*.

"Well, hey there!" Vanessa's greeting rose above the hushed conversation of the other moviegoers.

Without asking whether she was welcome, Vanessa staked out the other two seats in the row and motioned for Cindy to join her. "Imagine running into you guys here," Vanessa said all too cheerfully. "I never suspected that you were a beefcake fan, Olivia."

Olivia mumbled something inarticulate.

"I think I must be Harvey Schlembarger's biggest fan in the whole world," Vanessa gushed on. "He was Mr. Universe, you know."

"In about 1956," Cindy grumbled disloyally.

Vanessa ignored this. "And I hear he's dated just about every starlet in Hollywood. I can see why, too. He can have my number any time."

With that, the theater went black and the movie began. Olivia tried to watch the picture, but within minutes she was hopelessly confused. For one thing she couldn't figure out just who was the enemy that Vartan had set out to conquer. At first, she'd thought the setting was England. But the enemy queen wore a semitransparent gown of green sequined material that looked as if it came straight out of a *Star Trek* rerun. And the queen's army was composed of strange dwarflike creatures with pointy ears. Worse still, Vartan's loyal lieutenant and the actor who played the queen's chief henchman looked a lot alike, which made the fight scenes very confusing.

The action back in their row of seats was almost as complex. Not long after the movie started, Jimmy had all too casually rested his hand on top of Olivia's own. Then as the first fight scene reached its peak, the hand moved to Olivia's knee.

Olivia had stared at it as if it was some sort of exotic insect. Jimmy pretended not to notice, and began planning his next move.

The hand had just begun to squeeze Olivia's knee a bit more familiarly when Vanessa turned toward both of them to comment on the action. "Isn't this juicy," she said. "Don't you just find these battle scenes *riveting*."

Distracted and embarrassed, Jimmy returned to square one.

The same routine was repeated at least three times before he gave up in total defeat.

Vartan had better success. By the time the film ended, he had vanquished the empress's army and rescued a blonde Viking princess who had been held captive by a large mechanical bird in a cave.

As Vartan and his bride sailed off into the sunset in their Viking ship, Vanessa applauded enthusiastically. "Jimmy, I really hate to ask," she said, ignoring Olivia's presence entirely, "but do you suppose you could give Cindy and me a lift home? We both live just off Connell Drive. It isn't very far past Olivia's. Cindy's dad dropped us off here, and I was supposed to call my folks for the ride home. But I don't dare since it's so late."

"Uh, sure. Why not," Jimmy agreed.

At first, Olivia felt indignant. How had Vanessa and Cindy planned to get home if they hadn't run into her and Jimmy? Besides, it wasn't late at all. Just the normal time that the movie had been scheduled to end: shortly before ten. At least Vanessa could bother to think of a more logical excuse, Olivia thought.

As they piled into the Mustang, Olivia calmed down enough to savor the amusing side to the situation. No doubt it had never occurred to Vanessa that she was rescuing Olivia from an uncomfortable situation. It was probably the first good deed Vanessa had ever done in her life — consciously or not.

Not only had Vanessa's presence kept Jimmy at bay during the movie, but Olivia decided that it gave her the perfect excuse to end the date early. She'd already warned Jimmy that she wanted to be home before her mother returned that evening. And Vanessa and Cindy both lived a good bit farther from the mall than she did.

Olivia waited until they were about to turn into the entrance to Connell Drive before announcing her decision. "I guess you'd better let me off first," she said sweetly. "My mother doesn't like me to be late, any more than Vanessa's father does."

Jimmy, looking perplexed and totally defeated, let her off in her driveway and Olivia ran inside without a backward glance.

Inside the house, Mrs. Evans was waiting, home early from her meeting on purpose to monitor the time of her daughter's return. "You didn't mention that one of your friends was a boy," she said accusingly.

"I thought I did."

"Well, maybe you did say something," Mrs. Evans corrected herself, reluctant to let go of her suspicions. "But you shouldn't have gone out without a warm hat. You've got to watch your health."

"Mom! We were in the car or the theater the whole evening. I don't need a hat just to walk across a parking lot!"

"That's what *you* say, young lady. Suppose the car broke down on the road. Suppose you had an accident. What then?"

Olivia gave up. If she were in an accident, the last of her worries would be needing a hat. The first would be figuring out how to break the news to her mom without bringing on an hysterical scene.

Up in her room that night, Olivia tossed and turned, unable to sleep. Everyone said that high school was supposed to be the best time of your whole life — nothing but parties and laughs and good times. She wanted those good times. So why couldn't she just relax and enjoy herself? She was sure the problem must be unique.

CHAPTER

5

Vanessa wasted no time in informing the world of Olivia's date with Jimmy Hilbert.

The next day at lunch, she made a point of joining one of the crowded tables at the front of the cafeteria, setting her tray down immediately across from Olivia's old boyfriend, Michael.

"You'll never guess who I saw at the movies last night, taking in the last showing of *Vartan the Viking*," she announced to no one in particular.

"King Kong," someone suggested.

"Mrs. Oetjen," said someone else, naming Tarenton's principal. "She wants to revise the dress code and was taking notes."

Vanessa milked the suspense as long as possible, then dropped her bombshell. "Jimmy Hilbert and Olivia Evans! Can you believe it! Jimmy's so cool, and Olivia's such a little mouse! I wonder how she manages to keep Jimmy interested in her." Vanessa rolled her eyes wickedly, in case anyone present should miss the implications of her remarks.

But Michael, however he felt about the news, was not about to fall into Vanessa's trap. He peered across the table, studying Vanessa as if she were speaking a foreign language he'd only just begun to pick up. "Would you like my dessert?" he said after a long pause. "It's stewed prunes."

The boy seated beside Michael let out a loud guffaw, which was echoed the length of the table, as Michael's put-down began to sink in. Vanessa, slinging her hair over her shoulder in a demonstration of wounded dignity, picked up her tray and left in search of more appreciative company.

Only one person in the group had failed to see the humor in the incident. Nancy Goldstein, seated quietly at the far end of the table, was mulling over the meaning of Vanessa's revelation. Just last Friday she had confessed her interest in Jimmy. And on Tuesday Olivia Evans had gone out on a date with him. *Olivia*, of all people — Olivia, who rarely dated at all!

As far as Nancy was concerned, Olivia was a traitor. Why else would she pick out the one guy that Nancy had just developed an interest in, out of the hundreds at Tarenton High?

Choking with hurt and anger, Nancy grabbed her own tray and dumped the remains of her uneaten lunch into the nearest garbage bin. She had no idea where she was headed, but her homing instinct took her straight to her locker where she could at least recover her composure and undo the damage done to her makeup by the tears of rage that had welled up in her eyes. She combed her thick, dark hair and outlined her dark eyes. Feeling more composed, she decided to restrain her impulse to find Olivia and strangle her on the spot. Instead, she went back to the lunchroom and located Angie Poletti.

"Ange, can I talk to you?" she hissed.

"Sure thing."

Angie followed Nancy out into the hall. "What's wrong? You look just awful, Nancy," she said.

"Thanks." Nancy smiled wanly and repeated the story she'd just heard from Vanessa.

"I'm sure there's some explanation," Angie said after hearing the tale. "Let's not jump to conclusions."

"Like what?" Nancy demanded.

Angie searched her mind for possibilities. "Well, maybe she had already agreed to go out with Jimmy *before* Friday night," Angie suggested. "That would be different, wouldn't it? You couldn't expect her to break a date just because you mentioned liking him."

Even in her present mood, Nancy could see the logic of that. "But that wasn't the way it was," she insisted. "I remember Olivia saying right then that her social life was zero. She had nothing going for her at all. Why would she say that so definitely if she already had a date with Jimmy? Besides, for once Vanessa spoke the truth. Jimmy isn't Olivia's type at all. If anything, she's attracted to quiet, serious types like Michael. And Jimmy Hilbert is definitely *not* that kind."

Angie pondered the situation a little more, reluctant to see evil in anyone's motives. Except Vanessa's. . . .

"Vanessa!" Angie said aloud. "Has it occurred to you that Vanessa might have made the whole thing up? You know what a schemer she is!"

Nancy considered this. "I don't think so. I'm sure Vanessa was trying to stir up trouble by telling Michael what she saw, but I don't think it was a lie. For one thing, Jimmy would be furious with her if she made the whole story up. And Vanessa wouldn't want to have that happen. She'd never let herself get on the wrong side of a guy who drives a new Mustang."

Angie giggled. "I suppose you're right. That means there's only one explanation left — Olivia Evans is a creep."

Nancy arrived at cheerleading practice that afternoon, still boiling with anger but hoping that she could manage to get through the practice and save her grievances for a private talk with Olivia later on.

Changing hurriedly into her practice clothes, she entered the gym and joined the others who were already seated in a circle listening to a pep talk from Coach Engborg.

"I don't have to remind you," Ardith began, "that we've got the Grove Lake game coming up in a little less than two weeks. Now this is an important basketball game, not just for you students but for alumni as well, so we really want to be on our toes. Some of your parents and older brothers and sisters may recall, even if you don't, that Grove Lake used to be Tarenton's traditional grudge rival."

Ardith smiled at the looks of noncomprehension that went around the group. "That was back in the old days," she explained, "before 1963, when the conferences were reorganized. But a lot of us old folks still remember it. And you can bet that Grove Lake remembers — and the local newspapers and media, too. We might even get coverage of the game on TV news, so I want to make sure that our cheerleading squad is in top form."

Everyone looked suitably impressed, except possibly Walt, who had made bit appearances on his parents' TV show since he was three and was completely relaxed about appearing on camera.

At the other extreme, Mary Ellen was excited over the possibility of TV coverage. Even if the squad only appeared for a minute or so, she was determined to make the time count. "We'll need a new attack cheer," she pointed out to the others, "since we don't normally play Grove Lake during the regular season."

"Grove Lake's mascot is the grizzly bear," Walt mused. "So we will have to refer to that."

"How about 'Grind the Grizzlies'?" Mary Ellen suggested.

"Okay," Walt said encouragingly. "Go on. How will the rest of it go?"

Mary Ellen thought for a few seconds. "I don't know. Maybe 'Grind the Grizzlies. Mash 'em to a pulp. . . .' "

Olivia made a face. "Do we always have to have so much violence in our cheers?" she asked. "I mean, that's awfully *graphic*."

"It's an attack cheer," Mary Ellen said, exasperated. "What should we say: 'Hug the Grizzlies! Aren't they cute?' "

"No, of course not." Olivia looked ready to give up. "I just thought it might be nice to have some cheers that emphasize positive values."

"You mean like loyalty?" Nancy said sarcastically.

Everyone stared in her direction. No one knew what Nancy was talking about, but the challenge and hostility in her voice were unmistakable.

"Sure," Olivia said weakly. "Why not?"

"Because I don't think you know anything about the meaning of the word, that's why," Nancy retorted.

Ardith Engborg looked stern. "If this has to do with the squad, we'll hash out the problem right now," she announced. "If it's personal, I trust you two will be mature enough to settle the dispute between you. I won't have personal feuds getting in the way of our work."

Ardith left no doubt that she meant business. Nancy wilted a bit under her glare. "That's okay with me," she said, trying hard to keep her voice even. "I can wait till later."

"And you?" Ardith looked in Olivia's direction.

"Sure," she said in a tiny voice. "I don't even know what this is about."

With peace restored for the time being, at least, Ardith suggested that the squad work on a trick they had discussed in the past but never got around to trying. It involved the girls doing tumbling runs through a large hoop, held by Walt and Pres.

"When we actually do the trick," Ardith explained, "we'll have tissue paper stretched over the opening of the hoop. The first girl to do a forward roll through the hoop breaks the paper."

"Sounds great," Mary Ellen said. "It certainly will be a dramatic entrance onto the gym floor. But isn't it difficult to get through the hoop?"

Ardith shook her head. "It's much easier than it looks. And the two fellows holding the hoop make it easier still. They can adjust the position of the hoop a bit if it looks as if the tumbler is going to hit wrong. All it takes is a little cooperation on their part."

Cooperation, unfortunately, was not in the works between Walt and Pres that afternoon.

For three days in a row now Walt had sat in silent protest, never so much as picking up his pen during the journal-writing segment of Mr. Gaetano's class. If he had been anyone else, his passive resistance might not have attracted much attention. But Walt was accepted as a class leader, the catalyst of every prank and every new trend. His behavior was not only noticed, but it had distracted the rest of the class so much that very little journal writing was getting done by anyone. Most of the students scribbled something in their books just to get by, all the while devoting most of their attention to the silent battle of wills going on between Walt and Mr. Gaetano.

In the beginning, most of the class had been on Walt's side. He was well liked, and there was always a tendency — cruel perhaps, but all too human — to challenge a new teacher and enjoy studying him or her for signs of cracking under pressure. Every day, however, the mood of the class seemed to be moving slowly but perceptibly in the other direction. Mr. Gaetano was clearly a decent guy, and the better students were becoming annoyed with Walt for disrupting what could have been an interesting project.

Today, as the class period ended, Andrea Markley, one of the honor students, had gone up to Walt in the classroom and confronted him openly. "So, what's the point of all this?" she had asked. "If you want to flunk, go ahead and do it. We don't care. But at least put your name in the silly notebook. Or don't come to class at all."

For a second, Walt had been speechless. The fact was, his original reason for not writing in the journal had already begun to seem pointless. No matter how badly he wrote, he had nothing to lose. Total noncooperation was the way to a sure F. Somewhere along the line, however, his refusal to write had turned into a gesture. With a capital G.

Feeling too silly to tell the truth, Walt had searched around for some explanation for his behavior that Andrea might buy.

"I just don't think creative people can be forced to perform on cue," Walt had told her. "How can I be inspired to write sitting here in this dingy classroom? And if I did have a good idea, I wouldn't want to be interrupted by Gaetano's stopwatch, would I? It's stupid. The man just doesn't understand how creative minds work."

Andrea hadn't looked as if she thought much of his excuse. "Thinking that one up was your most creative act in months," she said, turning her back on Walt. But a few bystanders had seemed mildly impressed, and Walt had calculated that he had picked up at least a couple of new sympathizers.

In his own mind, though, he was in silent agreement with Andrea. His own parents were in television, and he knew very well that they got up every morning and did their show on time no matter what. Waiting for inspiration had nothing to do with it.

The fact was, Walt felt trapped. If he kept on his present course, he was sure to fail English. If he gave in, he'd look as if he were backing down. And Mr. Gaetano would have no reason whatsoever to give him a break in grading his lousy grammar. He was headed for disaster either way.

None of this made it any easier for him to concentrate during practice. The first time Angie came in too low for her forward roll through the hoop, Walt failed to respond to Pres's tug adjusting the hoop downward, and Angie's toe caught the lower edge of the hoop as she went through, pulling the hoop out of the boys' hands and sending it flying.

"Are you all right?" Walt asked Angie absentmindedly as she lay in a heap on the mat, the hoop tangled between her legs.

"I guess so," she laughed. "Just surprised, that's all."

"If you were paying attention, dummy, it would never have happened," Pres told Walt.

Pres's rebuke reminded Walt of their run-in the previous Friday, an incident he had almost forgotten in the wake of this classroom troubles. "Why don't you stop needling me," he shot back.

"All I want is for you to pay attention to what you're doing for a change," Pres groused.

"Look, I've had problems lately," Walt explained in a halfway sort of apology. "I can't help it."

Pres was unmollified. "Has it ever occurred to you that you aren't the only one with problems? Just because some of us don't put on a big act, doesn't mean we don't have difficulties, too."

"Come on, you guys," Angie said, jumping to her feet and moving between them. "It's no big deal. We can't do every trick right every time. I'm sure everyone's personal problems will get straightened out, too."

"That shows how much you know," Walt retorted. "It's your stupid cousin who's making my life miserable. And you think he's *so* wonderful! Maybe you'll change your mind when I get kicked off the squad on account of my grades, and you have to find a new guy to take my place."

Angie blinked in surprise. She was used to playing peacemaker in other people's quarrels, not to being a partisan herself. And being in a different English class from Walt, she had somehow managed to remain oblivious to the great journal-writing war between him and Gaetano.

"Walt's just sore because we finally got a teacher who won't give him A's for charm alone," Nancy put in, not helping things any.

"That doesn't even deserve a reply," Walt retorted. Then he added, on second thought, "Of course, if you had to get by on charm, Nancy Goldstein, you wouldn't get far."

Olivia, who had been strangely silent since her own run-in with Nancy, let out a burst of laughter.

"Come on, gang, let's bury the hatchet and get back to work," Angie pleaded. "We need every practice session we've got between now and the Grove Lake game."

For once, however, Angie's mediation attempt had no effect. Walt announced that he didn't feel like doing any more practice routines that day, and Nancy and Olivia all too readily agreed. Finally, giving in to the inevitable, Ardith Engborg suggested that they break up early for once. "Let's just write this practice off as a lost cause," she said wearily. "Perhaps by tomorrow we'll all be in a better mood."

"Poor Ardith," Pres said later, as he helped Mary Ellen into the passenger seat of his Porsche.

Mary Ellen was doubly surprised — first, that Pres had thawed in his recent coolness toward her enough to offer her a ride; second, that his sympathies seemed to be focused more on their long-suffering coach than on the imminent disaster facing the squad.

"I feel bad for Ardith, too," she agreed. "But what about us? Here we are facing the biggest game of the season, not to mention a chance to appear on TV, and it's all going to be ruined because we're bogged done in a lot of petty quarrels and personal problems."

"Maybe they're not so petty," Pres mused. "That's just *your* point of view."

That was easy for Pres to say, Mary Ellen thought. He left practice, jumped straight into this wonderful sports car, and headed for a mansion by the lake. Cheerleading was just a game for him, a way to pass his spare time and simultaneously infuriate his father, who hated the very idea of a Tilford heir making a spectacle of himself leading cheers.

"I don't see how you can say that," she finally protested aloud. "This is our big chance! Ardith said there will even be TV cameras at the game!"

"Big deal!" said Pres, unimpressed.

"Maybe that's how *you* feel about it," Mary Ellen retorted, "but it certainly matters to me."

She was glad that she'd asked Pres to let her

off on Spring Street, near her mother's office, instead of at her house. A lot of times she thought she was silly to be sensitive about living in a tacky, turquoise-painted, frame house in one of Tarenton's poorer neighborhoods. But a few minutes with Pres when he was in one of his haughty lord-of-the-manor moods always reminded her that she had good reason to be sensitive. If Pres thought appearing on TV, on a game that would be telecast all over the state, was unbearably small-time, she could imagine what he'd be thinking about her house and family!

"You wouldn't understand how I feel," Mary Ellen announced defensively, "but cheerleading is the most important thing in my life. It's important to all of us. Except, apparently, to you."

Pres wished he'd never brought the subject up. Mary Ellen only talked that way because she had nothing really important to worry about, he told himself. Only a week ago, he might have told anyone who asked that the most important thing in life was his car, or learning a new gymnastic trick, or even having a date with a sexy girl. When you were facing the break-up of your home, though, things like that no longer seemed to matter much on a scale of one to ten.

Unable to put his thoughts into words without sounding corny or mysterious, Pres decided to change the subject. "How's Patrick?" he asked innocently.

Mary Ellen was guarded. "Why do you want to know?"

"Good grief!" Pres sighed. "No reason. I was just making conversation."

"He's okay. We're still talking. No thanks to whoever went out of his way to tell Pat what I said on Friday night."

"Don't pin that on *me*," Pres said defensively.

But that was exactly what Mary Ellen was doing. Up until now, she'd felt that it must have been Olivia, or possibly one of the other girls. On second thought, however, she felt sure that Pres must be the creep. She wasn't sure why he would do something like that. Except that Pres's ego was so large, he probably wouldn't want Patrick to be dating her . . . even though he really didn't want her for himself.

"I'm not making any accusations," Mary Ellen lied, "but in the future, don't think you have to be my messenger. I can start enough arguments with Patrick without help from you."

The Porsche had just come down the hill onto Spring Street, three blocks of old-fashioned brick and stucco commercial buildings quite different from the rest of Tarenton, which was a picture-book pretty resort town. To Mary Ellen, Spring Street would always epitomize the small-town dullness of Tarenton. A store like Millie's Fashions managed to survive year after year, featuring a window display of mannequins draped in "house dresses" that Mary Ellen felt sure would have looked dumpy and old-fashioned forty years ago. Who wore such things? Someone must, since Millie's stayed in business. The brightest spots on the three-block long street were the two hardware stores — Olaffson's and Murtries, avid competitors who had stuffed their respective front windows with brightly colored displays of power tools, lawn mowers, and tractor accessories.

Pres is just a tourist in this world, Mary Ellen told herself. He drops by from his house on the peninsula when he feels like it. But his family doesn't know this street exists, you can be sure of that.

Pres's bland smile and his show-off moves as he steered the Porche one-handedly into a parking space between two old pickup trucks tried Mary Ellen's determination to say no more. "You think all of life is a joke," she blurted out accusingly, "but to some of us, it isn't!"

That did it! "Just because I don't go around whining all the time," Pres snorted, "everyone seems to think I have no feelings. And don't blame me for your problems with Patrick, Mary Ellen Kirkwood," he added. "You treat that guy like a yo-yo, reeling him in whenever it suits your purposes. I won't take the blame for your guilty conscience."

Mary Ellen was too furious to even think of a reply. Jumping out of the passenger seat, she slammed the door behind her hard — a move she knew was guaranteed to set Pres's teeth on edge. She headed off toward her mother's office without a backward glance. She didn't have to look back actually. She could tell from the sound of the Porsche, as Pres all but burned rubber making the turn back toward Route 21, that he was just as furious as she was.

As she entered the office of the Great North Insurance Company where her mother worked, Mary Ellen made sure that her face gave no hint that she was anything but totally carefree. Smiling broadly, she greeted Miss Petrasson, her mother's friend.

"You look beautiful as usual, Mary Ellen," Miss Petrasson said as she buzzed Mrs. Kirkwood in the back room to signal that it was time to leave for the day. "You make me wish I was back in high school, without a care in the world."

If she only knew! Mary Ellen thought. Why do all adults remember high school as four years of smooth sailing?

As she waited for her mother to gather up her things, Mary Ellen found herself counting off the problems that were dividing the squad:

Olivia and Nancy were feuding over Jimmy Hilbert.

Walt was angry with Angie because of his problems with Mr. Gaetano, her cousin.

Nancy was peeved with Walt because she felt the classroom stand-off was all his fault.

Pres was upset with Walt, and now with her, Mary Ellen. *Why* was a mystery, but then most things that went on in Pres's mind were a mystery to the rest of the world.

And now she was furious with Pres, since he must be the one who had gone out of his way to start a quarrel between her and Patrick.

Coach Engborg might kid herself that everyone's differences would get worked out in time for the play-off game, but Mary Ellen couldn't see any prospect of that. The feuding spirit seemed to be contagious, like an epidemic of chicken pox or flu. The squad was tearing itself apart.

CHAPTER

Nancy Goldstein had already considered her priorities. Which came first, squad loyalty or Jimmy Hilbert? The answer did not take long for her to figure out. "Loyalty is worthless unless it's a two-way street," she told Angie Poletti. "The squad can fall apart for all I care. I won't take Olivia's betrayal lying down."

In fact, Nancy was physically lying down as she spoke, stretched out on her bed simultaneously watching a rock video on MTV, blow drying her hair, and talking on the telephone to Angie. After years of being dimly aware of rock music at best, she had become an avid fan during her romance with Alex, the British exchange student who had played with a local new wave band. The drawn out routine of washing, conditioning, and styling her hair was a bad sign, though. Nancy was one of those girls who got compulsive about her hair when she was depressed.

"Don't you think you're jumping to conclusions?" Angie was arguing, raising her voice to compete with the whine of Nancy's blow dryer. "You should at least try to talk this out with Olivia before you condemn her. There's probably a good explanation."

Angie had a steady boyfriend and could afford to be philosophical on the subject of jealousy.

Nancy didn't see matters so coolly. "What explanation could there be?" she wondered aloud. "I've even been inviting Olivia to my parties, and seeing that others invite her, too. All for the sake of the squad. How can you make excuses for her? She's trying to steal my new boyfriend right out from under my nose!"

"I'm not making excuses," Angie explained patiently. "I'm just suggesting that a six-foot-three, 190-pound male isn't that easy to steal . . . unless he *wants* to be stolen."

Nancy didn't want to hear what Angie was trying to tell her. "It's just *got* to work out with Jimmy," she wailed. "He's the first guy my folks have approved of right from the start, since I came to Tarenton."

"I don't get it," Angie objected. "Since when has parent-appeal been a must quality in guys?"

"Since lately. For me, at least. I'm tired of battling with my mom and dad all the time."

Angie giggled. "It's funny to think of Jimmy Hilbert being any parent's dream. The word is, he has fast hands, and I don't mean just on the basketball court."

"It's true, too," Nancy laughed. "But I can handle that."

There was a long silence on the other end of the line. "So how come your folks like him? He isn't Jewish. Or is he?"

It tickled Nancy that the issue of being Jewish, so crucial to her parents, was a total mystery to Angie. For months her new friend had gone on the assumption that Nancy Goldstein was Catholic.

"No, Angie, he isn't," Nancy explained. "But that's the only strike against him. Otherwise, he's my parents' dream: a preppy dresser, a smooth talker, and his father happens to be a prominent lawyer who's active in politics and writes articles for national environmental publications. If that isn't enough, Mrs. Hilbert graduated from the University of Michigan, just as my mom did, and they're both active in alumni affairs."

"It's hard to imagine Jimmy Hilbert being the son of two real go-getters," Angie mused. "He isn't the studious type, that's for sure."

"So?" Nancy objected. "I'm studious enough for both of us."

After she had hung up the phone, Nancy switched off the blow dryer and lay back on her peach-colored bedspread, staring at the ceiling. It was probably true that her parents liked Jimmy even better than she did. From that point of view, it wasn't such an ideal romance. But she *was* tired of fighting every battle with her parents. Mom and Dad weren't ogres. They usually gave in when she truly wanted something, and they liked her friends well enough when they got to know them. But being an only child wasn't easy. Her folks had such high expectations. Nancy couldn't help envying Mary Ellen and Angie, who had younger siblings to distract their folks' attention once in a while.

Of course, that's the way life worked, Nancy reflected. If you wanted anything, you had to be a fighter. So why was she holed up in her room moping about Jimmy? Why not take the initiative?

On impulse, Nancy reached for the phone again and dialed Jimmy Hilbert's number.

She hadn't figured out what she was going to say. If she'd bothered to think out her strategy ahead of time, she'd have lost her nerve. So when Jimmy's voice answered, she just blurted out the first suggestion that came to mind.

"I called because we have this history quiz tomorrow," she explained into the mouthpiece.

"We do? Oh, yeah."

Nancy found Jimmy's total indifference to schoolwork exciting but a bit scary.

"It's on the Civil War, remember?" Nancy reminded him.

"Well, who won?"

"The north, silly," Nancy giggled.

"Great," Jimmy said. "Now that we have that out of the way, how would you like to go skiing tonight? They have night skiing up at Brinley Mountain."

"Sure. Let's live dangerously."

Nancy was sure her mother would say no. But she was wrong. Telling her that the invitation came from Jimmy Hilbert worked wonders. Permission was granted.

Nancy didn't go skiing often, but before her last outing she'd bought a new ski suit that she was eager to show off. The pink stretch pants and pink and gray jacket were topped off with a matching striped cap that showed off her thick, dark hair to advantage. Jimmy's reaction, when he picked her up on her doorstep a little later, told her that she looked as good as she felt.

It took less than an hour to get to Brinley Mountain. Only one intermediate slope was flood-lighted for night skiing, but it was a good run, just tough enough for Nancy to demonstrate her skills. The crowd was mostly made up of college kids from the state university nearby, and there weren't too many of them. By nine-thirty, Nancy and Jimmy were completing their second good run of the night.

"Whew! That was terrific!" Nancy exclaimed, as she caught up with Jimmy at the bottom of the hill after a brisk second run. "Didn't I do great? Did you see my form on the big turn up at the top?"

"Your form is great all the time, if you ask me," Jimmy said, looking at the way her figure filled the skintight ski pants.

Nancy made a face. She was beginning to find Jimmy's need to make comments like that a real turn-off. Not that she was a prude, but there was something insincere about the way Jimmy kept pushing the subject of sex constantly. Like he was trying to prove something.

"What you need is to cool off," she joked out loud. Scooping up a handful of snow, she fashioned a crude snowball.

Jimmy pretended to run away, but soon let himself be caught.

Nancy playfully lobbed the snowball at his chest, and giggling, let herself be tackled into the bank of soft snow that lay piled against the side of the ski lodge.

After a few seconds of mock tussling she was ready to get up. But not Jimmy. He seemed determined to turn the game into an impromptu grope session.

Out of the corner of her eye, Nancy noticed that two college guys passing by on their way to the refreshment stand were staring at them with funny smirks on their faces. "Youth," one of the guys said in a loud voice. "I sure do miss it!"

His friend laughed and stared harder.

"Jimmy!" Nancy hissed. "Good grief, let me go. Not here. It's gross."

Jimmy ignored her protests and kissed her hard. Nancy was aware that her heart didn't beat faster, and all she could think of was that he was being a jerk.

Then he let her go and stood up, laughing, not

caring that Nancy had not been responsive to him. "Well, how about a hamburger, then, before we head home."

Inside the high-ceilinged lodge, Nancy and Jimmy found a table and ordered burgers and fries. Ravenous from the exercise, Nancy polished off the food with no trouble at all, while Jimmy conducted a monologue on his other favorite topic — himself.

To hear Jimmy tell it, he was about to write a new chapter in the history of Tarenton basketball. Hank had never been as good a center as everyone thought. In a way, his injury was a stroke of luck for everyone. Come the Grove Lake game, Jimmy would show everyone that he had deserved to be in the starting lineup all along.

Nancy pushed the remnants of her French fries around her plate and yawned.

Jimmy was the perfect guy for her in so many ways, she scolded herself. The two of them made a great-looking couple. Her parents were putty in his hands. She usually found him very sexy . . . at least she would if he'd only stop pushing so hard and let her feel that it was partly her own idea.

So how could she spoil it all by admitting to herself that there were times when she found him to be a big bore?

Annoyed with herself, Nancy pushed the thought to the back of her mind. She decided that she wasn't going to bring up the subject of

Jimmy's movie date with Olivia either. They weren't going steady or anything like that, so why make a fuss? Maybe when they got to know each other better, her doubts would evaporate. For now, she'd just keep quiet and hope for the best.

When he stopped his car in front of her house, Nancy put her arms around his neck when he kissed her, letting herself enjoy the feelings he could arouse in her when they had some privacy.

CHAPTER

7

The squad's Friday afternoon practice was turning out to be even more of a disaster than Wednesday's had been.

At first, Mary Ellen had thought that everyone was settling down to work. But the trouble started when Olivia made a sarcastic remark about Nancy's awkward attempt at a split at the end of the "We're number one!" cheer.

"It's supposed to look easy," Olivia said, as Nancy hauled herself up off the floor, grimacing with the effort.

Mary Ellen couldn't decide who to sympathize with. She herself didn't find splits that easy and felt a good deal of envy over Olivia's ability to turn herself into a pretzel at will. On the other hand, Nancy did seem out of shape today.

The explanation wasn't long in coming. "Sorry, everyone," Nancy groaned. "I went skiing the other night and now my muscles are getting their revenge."

This was no news to Olivia. Although Jimmy hadn't mentioned the ski trip to her, Vanessa had been quick to notice the lift tag on his jacket the next day and point it out just when she knew Olivia would overhear.

Olivia had promised herself that she wouldn't say a thing to Nancy. She didn't want to get in a jealous snit. But Nancy's bringing the subject up right to her face was the final straw.

"Maybe your social life is starting to interfere with the squad," Olivia huffed.

Nancy felt defensive. She hadn't meant the excuse as a dig at Olivia, but Olivia's criticism went too far.

"My social life is my own business," she snapped.

"Does anyone mind if we get back to work?" Ardith intervened. "There's going to be an important game next weekend, whether you all have your personal lives in order or not."

"How can we go through our drill without Walt?" Angie wondered aloud. "He's twenty minutes late."

"He should be here soon," Ardith said.

It seemed that earlier that day in Mr. Gaetano's class, Walt had complained out loud that he couldn't possibly write in his journal with so many people around. He needed privacy. So Mr. Gaetano had offered to solve that problem by making Walt stay after school every day for twenty minutes of detention. The sentence was to last until he wrote at least one paragraph in his journal for every day he'd missed so far.

No sooner had Ardith finished explaining this than there was a commotion outside in the hall. The double doors of the gym swung open and Walt backed through them, waving good-bye to a group of cheering freshmen out in the hall.

Then he turned around and proudly displayed to the squad the reason for the laughs he'd been getting. His bright orange T-shirt bore the custom-lettered motto: FREE WALT MANNERS.

Pres, Mary Ellen, and Olivia couldn't help laughing.

Angie felt her heart sink to her feet. She could just imagine what her cousin Tom had thought of this gesture. Walt had always liked to play the role of the rebel and class jester. But up to now, he'd never let his little jokes go too far. If he had to get involved in something like this, why had he decided to pick on a nice guy like Tom?

It was Nancy who put into words some of what Angie was feeling. Relieved to be distracted from the awkward situation with Olivia, which she didn't really know how to handle, she turned her annoyance on Walt.

"I, for one, don't see the joke," she said. "If you want to express yourself, all you have to do is write something in your journal. *Anything.* What's the big deal?"

It was easy for Nancy to talk, Walt thought. She got A's without even trying.

"Thanks for the support, Nancy," Walt drawled. "I knew I could count on you."

"Enough!" Ardith's one word comment left no doubt that she meant business. "Back to work, and I don't want a single other interruption this afternoon."

The squad did manage to get in a straight half hour of practice after that. They went through some of their old cheers and then Walt started to teach a new halftime routine he'd worked out that involved a series of break dancing moves. He and Pres loved the routine because for once, they got to do flashy, acrobatic moves instead of just lifting and supporting the girls.

Mary Ellen was a bit less enthusiastic. Walt had long ago perfected his Michael Jackson imitation and was constantly looking for ways to work it into their routines. By now, the others had pretty much caught up with him. When they moved their feet, it looked as if they were gliding on roller skates. Mary Ellen was the only one on the squad who couldn't seem to get the hang of the moves. She knew she looked ridiculous.

Fortunately for Mary Ellen's ego, Nancy was having problems today, too. Every time the steps called for a sideways kick she grunted in agony. Her muscles were so stiff from skiing that she could barely move.

If I look like someone trying to swim out of the water, Mary Ellen thought, Nancy looks like a windup toy soldier.

"What a pair you two make! I love it!" The derisive comment echoed Mary Ellen's thoughts exactly. Startled, she looked toward the door of the gym just in time to see Donny Henderson taking her and Nancy's picture with a telephoto lens.

"Perfect!" Donny crowed again. "Mary Ellen's expression couldn't have been better. The agony and embarrassment of being caught in the act!"

"Would you care to explain what you're doing?" Ardith snapped. "No one said anything about taking yearbook pictures today. We're trying to work."

Donny, who was in charge of yearbook photography, was not used to being challenged. "We just need a few candid shots," he explained unabashedly.

Coach Engborg looked none too pleased. "Does it have to be now?" she asked, giving in. "We've got work to do."

"Oh, don't mind us," Donny said. "Just go right ahead. That's the whole point. We don't want poses. We want to show a glimpse of the hard work that goes into putting your great routines together."

Angie and Pres, standing safely out of Ardith's view, rolled their eyes in appreciation of Donny's line. He could really sling it.

"Well, I suppose it's all right," Ardith agreed. "Just don't get in our way."

Mary Ellen, meanwhile, was slowly taking in just what Donny had meant by the use of the word *we*. Behind him, with another camera slung around his neck, was Patrick. Bad enough that she had just been captured in the most embarrassing photo of all time, but Patrick seemed to be finding the whole situation wildly amusing. She felt the blood flow to her cheeks.

For the rest of the practice, Mary Ellen did her best to ignore Patrick's presence. It wasn't easy, though, with him darting in and out of the line to snap pictures every few minutes. More than once, he pointed his camera right in Mary Ellen's face and snapped away. The more flustered she got, the more he seemed to be enjoying himself.

When Ardith finally called a merciful end to the session, Mary Ellen made straight for the locker room and changed into her street clothes as fast as she could manage it. She was planning to escape through the other door that led from the girls' locker room directly into the downstairs hall. But Patrick had anticipated that and was waiting for her when she emerged, leaning against the lockers that lined the opposite wall.

"Gotcha!" he laughed. He caught her in his arms and just held her, close to him. She felt the warmth of his body and the nice smell of his aftershave lotion. He didn't try to kiss her, just enclose her in his arms.

When he released her and saw her surprise at being caught, he said, "You can't escape me, you know."

"Apparently not," Mary Ellen said coolly.

"So why keep trying?" Patrick asked. He was smiling, but he was serious.

"I thought we agreed to just be friends," Mary Ellen replied. "If this is your idea of how to go about it, it's not a very good one."

"Okay, I admit that," Patrick said. "But we never agreed to stop talking. You've hardly said a word to me since we made that agreement."

"It's only been a couple of days," Mary Ellen pointed out.

"But it seems like centuries to me," Patrick countered. "It feels like the next ice age has started."

She gave him a look that said, "you're crazy." But Patrick was not about to let her off that easy. As she started past him, he reached out and held her by the arm.

"I wouldn't bother you, you know, if I didn't know that you really like me, in spite of how hard you try to pretend otherwise."

"What makes you think I like you?" Mary Ellen said, but the words were not very convincing. The pressure of Patrick's hand on her arm made her forget the meaning of "friends." His touch always did that. And she knew he felt it, too.

Patrick moved even closer and Mary Ellen felt what resistance she had left begin to melt away. He kissed her sweetly, tenderly, and she let him. But when she pulled away, her glance fell on Patrick's T-shirt. Back in the gym it had been partially hidden by the camera gear he wore around his neck. Now she could see the words printed across his chest: HENLEY TRASH.

Involuntarily, she made a face of disapproval.

"What's wrong with my shirt?" Patrick said. "If Walt can advertise his silly games, I can wear this."

"I didn't say anything," Mary Ellen protested.

"You don't have to." For once, Patrick decided, he was going to speak his mind. "You know damn well that if my dad's business was Tarenton Fabricators, you wouldn't mind me wearing a shirt that said so."

"I don't know what you're talking about."

"Yes you do, Mary Ellen. Be honest."

Mary Ellen felt miserable. Why did Patrick insist on forcing the issue?

"I just want you to know that I'm not ashamed of my dad, or our business. Why should I be? He and Mom got married when they were just seventeen years old. They couldn't even afford to have an apartment of their own. And now my dad has his own business. What's wrong with that?"

"Nothing," Mary Ellen said honestly, "for *them*."

"For anyone," Patrick countered.

"Even the part about getting married at seventeen?" Mary Ellen wanted to know.

"Why not? If you're in love."

"That's fine if you want to spend the rest of your life right here in Tarenton. Raising babies and paying bills."

Mary Ellen pulled her arm from Patrick's grasp and strode down the hall, leaving him standing there looking after her. From his point of view, paying bills and raising babies was just part of life. Ordinary, everyday life. It didn't mean not being happy. Mary Ellen had a way of making the prospect sound like some sort of prison sentence.

And to Mary Ellen, that's just what it was.

Grabbing her coat from her locker, Mary Ellen ran out of the school building and headed toward the public bus stop. As always, she did her best to put the confrontation with Patrick out of her mind. She knew exactly what she wanted out of life, and for the most part her plans were right on course. She planned to go straight from high school to New York. She would break into high fashion modeling there. Maybe she'd even try working in Europe for a while, if she could manage it. And in the meantime, she'd take acting lessons.

None of this agenda seemed the least bit doubtful to her, until she let herself get distracted by Patrick. Being with him always made her feel confused and flustered. Not only were his plans completely incompatible with hers, but he was the one guy she knew who was every bit as determined to have his way as she was.

Mary Ellen was grateful when the bus pulled up ahead of schedule and she could get on board, leaving school behind for one more day.

The bus, just like the one her own father drove for a living, was always a reminder of the part of her life she wanted to leave behind. Settling into one of the rear seats, Mary Ellen reached into her bag and pulled out a copy of *Pizzazz*, her favorite fashion magazine, and began to study the full-color layouts. One featured a spread of slinky, hand-beaded evening dresses. Another showed five models with short, upswept hairdos demonstrating all-white play clothes by one of the avant-garde Japanese designers. There was no reason in the world why Mary Ellen couldn't be modeling clothes like these some day. And living the life that went with it. She was *not* going to let Patrick ruin that dream for her, no matter how attractive he was.

Patrick, meanwhile, was dropping off his camera equipment at the yearbook office when he ran into Vanessa Barlow.

"Hi there," Vanessa said, eyeing his camera. "Are you going to take my picture for the yearbook?"

Dressed in simple white shorts and a tennis team jersey, Vanessa was headed for her after-school lesson on the indoor court.

"Sure, why not?" Patrick agreed.

"How's this?" Standing sideways to Patrick, Vanessa cradled her racquet in one arm and looked over her shoulder at the camera lens.

It was hardly a candid shot, Patrick thought, but why argue. He focused the camera and snapped the shutter.

"Thanks," Vanessa said as she prepared to go on her way. "Oh, by the way, that's a cute T-shirt."

"Glad someone likes it," Patrick growled.

If he hadn't been feeling so low about Mary Ellen, maybe he would have been more cautious. Mary Ellen was just afraid of being trapped in Tarenton, but Vanessa was a grade-A snob.

Normally, her reactions to guys were in direct proportion to their importance or their family's bank balance. For the moment, however, Patrick let himself forget this.

"I don't suppose you happen to be free for next week's dance?" he said, turning up his Patrick Henley charm to full volume.

"Is that an invitation?" Vanessa asked casually. Needless to say from her reaction, she didn't have a date yet.

"You bet it is."

"It's a deal," Vanessa said in a low, husky voice.

"Great. We'll go to the game together and then hit the dance from there," Patrick said.

Whistling happily, Patrick locked up the photography storage room and left the school, headed for his late afternoon stint of work on his trash collection route. He felt triumphant. He had figured out a way to make Mary Ellen suffer for her attitude. Imagine how jealous she'd be when she saw him out with another girl — and Vanessa Barlow of all people! The girl she really hated.

Not that he was dumb enough to think that Vanessa was honestly interested in his company. No doubt she had some reason of her own for wanting to go to the dance with him. But that had nothing to do with him.

CHAPTER

"Angie, hurry up and don't forget to bring that salad that's in the refrigerator. And Papa's present, too."

Angie, who was already carrying three dozen homemade cookies, her snow boots, and her brother's eyeglasses, which had been left behind on the coffee table, stuffed the salad bowl into a shopping bag, grabbed her grandfather's birthday present, and staggered downstairs to the garage where her mother and brothers were waiting for her.

She didn't really mind spending her Friday evening with the family, celebrating her grandfather's seventy-fifth birthday. Her only regret was that Marc was not going to be home this weekend to attend the family party with her.

She'd been counting on seeing Marc, only to face disappointment when he had called earlier this afternoon to cancel the trip.

"Sorry, Ange," he had explained, "you know I'm dying to get home. But my electrical engineering prof gave us a whole batch of problems to work out by Monday."

"Can't you do them here?" Angie had asked.

"Not really. I need to use the computer lab. Sorry, but school's got to come first. Otherwise, there's no point in my being here."

Angie knew that it was useless to argue. Marc had been lucky to be able to go away to college at all. It was his big chance to escape a life of dead-end jobs, like the one servicing vending machines that he'd had when he and Angie first met. Besides, she'd broken dates with Marc for reasons a lot less important than studying. Her commitment to the cheerleading squad, for example. So she was just getting a dose of her own medicine.

"I'll miss you, Marc," she said, accepting the inevitable.

"Same here, baby. You know I miss you."

"Well, there's always next weekend," Angie said consolingly. "You'll be here for the Grove Lake game and the dance, won't you?"

There was a pause on the other end of the line. "I can't make any promises right now," Marc said finally. "I'm sorry, Ange. But these courses I'm taking are tough. It's hard to predict how much work I'll have, even a week in advance."

"Sure. I understand," Angie agreed.

She did understand, too. But understanding didn't stop her from being worried. Marc had a whole other life at college. She knew he loved her.

Right now. But could any romance last when the two people involved were so far apart, with different schedules and different responsibilities? She wasn't sure.

At least, Angie told herself, her grandfather's party would give her something to do tonight. Anything was better than sitting home and moping about Marc. By the time the Polettis' car pulled up in her grandparents' driveway, she was actually starting to look forward to her evening.

Grandfather and Grandmother DeAngelo — their family called them Papa and Mama — lived in a frame house surrounded by two acres of land, just beyond the city limits. Though not exactly a farm, Papa and Mama's place had always seemed like one to Angie when she visited there as a child. In those days, Mama had kept laying chickens and sold eggs at a nearby farm stand. Papa had raised rabbits.

The story of Papa's rabbits was one he never got tired of retelling every time the family got together, and tonight would be no exception.

"You look beautiful, Angie," Papa said, greeting her from his favorite reclining chair in the living room.

Angie put down her armloads of stuff and gave Papa a hello kiss.

An assortment of a dozen or so aunts, uncles, and cousins was already gathered in the room around Papa's chair, and sure enough he wasted no time regaling them with his favorite story about Angie. "When this one was small," he chuckled, "she loved to feed my rabbits. She was crazy about them. Then one day she found out that my customers didn't buy them for pets; rabbit stew was more what they had in mind. Little Angie didn't say anything at the time. But the next morning when I came out to feed the rabbits, they were all gone. Angie had gotten up before dawn and opened the doors of the cages."

Papa laughed at the memory. Though he'd been angry at the time, he'd later decided to give up selling rabbits altogether. "To me, there was nothing wrong with it," he explained, laughing at the memory, "but I couldn't have my own little granddaughter thinking I was a bunny killer." He looked at Angie with affection. "She's tenderhearted, this one."

Angie grinned in embarrassment and moved into the kitchen where her mother and her brother Andrew were already helping Mama set the table.

"At least we won't go hungry," her mother said in understatement, surveying the covered dishes that were arrayed on every counter and tabletop. Mama DeAngelo had been cooking all week, and the relatives hadn't arrived empty-handed either. There were baking dishes filled with lasagna and manicotti, loaves of garlic bread ready for the oven, a cold seafood salad, a veal roast, and assorted other goodies too tempting for diet-conscious Angie even to allow herself to think about.

If it weren't for the menu, Angie thought, you'd never guess that this family was Italian. Mama and Papa's offspring ranged in looks from honey-blonde, green-eyed Angie to the black hair and olive complexion of the Gaetano branch of the family. But there was something else the family had in common, too, even if it wasn't visible to the eye. They were very close-knit. No one in the family had been particularly surprised, years ago, when Papa gave up his rabbit business to keep from hurting the feelings of a little granddaughter who loved animals. It was taken for granted that every member of the family looked out for the happiness of all the others.

That was the reason that Angie didn't hesitate to take aside her cousin Tom for a talk. She felt sure that if only they could talk the situation over, the two of them could work out some solution to the Walt Manners problem.

Fifteen years older than Angie, Tom Gaetano had always been her favorite cousin. Though barely five-foot-ten, he'd been a basketball star in high school and college, known for his gung-ho attitude and his jumping ability, which made up for his height. He and his wife Sandy were high school sweethearts who'd managed to keep their romance going, even though they waited to marry until Tom had completed his master's degree and a hitch in the Army. Just looking at them now, happily married with two cute daughters, Angie felt reassured that there was some hope for her and Marc.

Confidently, she sought out Tom before dinner and found him in the basement playroom, keeping an eye on his little girls while discussing basketball with Uncle Ernie and Aunt Alice.

"What do you think of Tarenton's chances against Grove Lake?" Ernie was asking Tom.

Tom shook his head. "Not so hot. It looks as if Hank Vreewright is out for the rest of the year."

Angie joined her aunt on the couch. "But aren't you forgetting Jimmy Hilbert?" she asked. "He looked great in last week's game."

Uncle Ernie shook his head. "A hot dog if I ever saw one."

"He's right," Tom agreed. "Jimmy's one-man show worked for a few minutes, but it won't be enough to stop Grove Lake. They're a well-coached team, and it won't take them long to figure out that Jimmy hates to give up the ball. They'll make sure he's so fenced in that he never gets within shooting distance."

Angie was surprised. The kids she knew at school were so euphoric about last week's victory that they hadn't stopped to think that Jimmy's magic might not work a second time. When you thought about it though, you could see that Tom and Ernie's logic made sense.

In the meantime, though, there was something else she needed to discuss with Tom. "Can I talk to you alone for a minute?" she asked her cousin. "It's about school."

"Sure." Tom retreated with Angie to a pair of chairs in the far corner of the room.

"It's about Walt Manners," Angie began.

"Speaking of showboats, he's another," Tom said, making a face. "Don't worry, Angie, he's not going to ruin my enjoyment of teaching. If it comes down to a contest of wills, you can be sure of who'll win. I'm the one who gives out the grades in the end."

"Does that mean Walt will flunk English?" Angie asked, aghast. If he did, that would be disaster for the squad, not to mention Walt personally.

"He sure will if he keeps on the way he's been going," Tom said.

"But that's awful!" Angie exclaimed. "Can't you give him another chance? Walt's my friend. I'm sure there's just some misunderstanding between the two of you."

"You're damn right there's a misunderstanding! Walt thinks he can get away with murder. And if I let him, my chances for getting any respect as a teacher are nil."

The look in Tom's eyes reminded Angie of the temper she knew he had.

"I really don't believe that Walt meant to get into a battle with you," Angie said more calmly. "I know he must have had a reason for not wanting to keep a journal, even though I don't know what it was. And I'm sure that from there things just got out of hand. I bet he'd give anything right now to end this whole argument, if he could just do it without backing down in front of the whole class."

Tom considered this possibility. "You're probably right," he agreed, "but I'm not responsible for Walt's problem. I'm ready and willing to let him make up the assignments he's missed so far. But I can hardly let the rest of the class think that Walt is going to get away with writing nothing and still pass English. That wouldn't be fair to them. And it would make it completely impossible for me to demand any work from my classes in the future. There's no way I can save Walt from having to admit that he's in the wrong."

"Tom! Angie! Everyone! Dinner is ready!" Sandy's call from upstairs brought the conversation to an abrupt halt.

The only good thing that could be said for the rest of the evening was that Angie, for once, had no appetite for all the fattening food that was on the table. The knotted up feeling in her stomach came from the fact that she knew Tom was basically right. She'd been counting on him to come up with some magical solution that would end Walt's problems and save the squad. But this time there was no magical solution. When the grading period ended two weeks from now, Walt would have an F on his record, and his cheerleading days would be over.

On Saturday morning, Angie woke up at six A.M. and took a long, luxurious shower. She still hadn't thought of a solution to Walt's troubles, but she felt more optimistic than she had the night before, if only because things always looked brighter in the early morning hours.

Her father had been killed in an accident when Angie was a baby, and she had always taken over a heavy share of the responsibilities for running the house and looking out for her younger brothers. Her mother, busy running the beauty salon that she operated out of the small shop on the lower level of the Polettis' split-level house, relied on Angie to keep the household going.

Angie had never minded the responsibility, but she had soon gotten into the habit of getting up earlier than the rest of her family, just to give herself a few hours of privacy. In fact, the only good part about Marc's not being home for the weekends was that she wasn't staying out late with him and missing out on her only chance to spend time on herself, free from the demands of her family. She had a full schedule of errands planned for later that day, so this morning she intended to make the most of her private time.

Quickly drying herself after the shower, Angie pulled on her running pants, sweatshirt, and down vest. In the kitchen she gulped down a glass of orange juice while tying up her running shoes. As she headed down the outside steps and up the road, she couldn't help thinking how shocked Mary Ellen and some of the other girls at school would be if they knew that she, Angie Poletti, was a secret jogger.

In spite of her being a cheerleader, which belonged in a different category, Angie had always been the first to joke about how she was too lazy to enjoy any kind of physical exercise. Most of her friends took it for granted that Angie's athletic ability just came naturally, without any effort on her part.

In fact, Angie had started jogging reluctantly, knowing that it was either exercise or give up the chocolate and rich food she loved. She was still less than fanatical about the sport. But after a while, she'd come to look forward to her solitary morning runs.

On this particular morning, the air was clear and cold. Twenty minutes after leaving home, Angie had reached her goal — a small town park that sat on the hill overlooking the old downtown section of Tarenton. As usual the park was empty in the early morning hours, and Angie circled the paved pathway that ran along the promenade, enjoying the view of the village below. After her second time around the path, she felt she deserved a rest and plopped down on a bench, her eyes closed in a moment of solitary meditation.

The moment ended all too abruptly with the feeling of a wet, slobbery tongue licking at Angie's face. Blinking in shock, Angie opened her eyes in time to see a very large and very friendly labrador retriever in the process of settling himself right in her lap.

"*Freddie!* Mind your manners!" shouted the dog's owner, Kerry Elliot.

Freddie grudgingly moved off Angie's lap and settled between the two girls on the bench, blissfully unaware that in the opinion of some, dogs belonged on the ground.

Kerry gave the dog a fond look. "He's so spoiled. I know I should lay down the law sometimes, but I just can't stand to say no."

"That's okay." Angie was glad to see Kerry. Although she'd been disappointed when Kerry decided to stop going with her brother Andrew, she liked the way Kerry had managed things so that she and Andrew were still friends.

"How's everything with you?" Angie asked.

"Oh, fine," Kerry said, unconvincingly.

Angie had figured as much. She knew very well that Pres Tilford was the real reason Kerry had stopped going with Andrew. Pres had come on really strong about Kerry. It had even seemed that, for once in his life, he had lost his head over a girl. But lately, he'd been acting awfully strange.

Based on Pres's past history, Angie felt she knew the story. Pres had changed his mind yet again, and now Kerry was feeling betrayed and depressed. It was so typical of Pres.

"Oh, that's not it at all," Kerry insisted after Angie had gently questioned her about Pres.

"It isn't?" Angie was more confused than ever. "So what's gone wrong?"

Kerry sighed and began filling Angie in on the scene that had taken place in the Tilford library.

"I was so upset at being called a floozy," Kerry admitted. "I guess it bothered me because I know Pres's reputation. I don't want to end up as just another girl that Pres Tilford loved and left.

"Now that I've thought things over, though, I realize it wasn't Pres's fault," Kerry went on. "He can't help what his mother says, and she *had* been drinking. But I'm not sure I'm going to get a chance to talk it over with him. I told him to take me home and wouldn't talk about it. Ever since then, he's been avoiding me."

"You have to talk to him, Kerry," Angie said. "But at least now I know why Pres has been strange recently. Family problems can make people weird."

After Kerry and Freddie left, Angie sat for a while on the park bench, thinking over what she'd just learned. In theory, there was no reason why she should be interested in helping Pres and Kerry get back together.

Still, Pres was her friend. It bothered her to think that, like everyone else, she'd accepted his golden boy image as the whole truth. How could anyone as handsome and rich and *lucky* as Pres have problems?

Now, as it turned out, Pres seemed to have problems that made the rest of their troubles seem petty. Walt's feud with her cousin Tom, the cheerleading squad's difficulties, even her own tendency to feel sorry for herself at having to get through the weekend without Marc, didn't amount to much after all. Pres was the one with *real* troubles.

CHAPTER

If Pres Tilford lived in the biggest house in town, Walt Manners inhabited the most unusual one.

Located deep in the woods outside town, the Manners' house was an architect-designed contemporary fantasy, complete with an entire glass wall with a view of the woods and distant Narrow Brook Lake; a kitchen illuminated by a huge skylight; and a big, airy room, over the studio his parents used for broadcasting, which Walt had turned into a cozy hideaway for himself.

Modern as it was, however, the Manners' house came equipped with old-fashioned, wood burning stoves. And stoves needed fuel to burn. So that's how it happened that Walt had become quite an expert at chopping wood, a chore his parents had turned over to him as soon as he was old enough to manage an ax safely.

One thing about cutting wood was it gave Walt a chance to think out his problems. On this particular Saturday, as he attacked the problem of reducing a large pile of logs to firewood, he was also mentally dissecting his own situation.

Even though he was only wearing a thin flannel shirt, Walt had managed to work up a good sweat, partly because of the heat generated by his hard work. But at the moment, Walt would have been plenty hot even if he had been standing still. The dull thwacking sound of the ax as it bit into the logs usually had a calming effect. Today, Walt felt himself getting more agitated the longer he worked.

Walt had started out feeling sore that he should be in all this trouble over his little problems with spelling and grammar. No one outside of school considered these things important. Walt knew that his own father was a less than perfect speller, and this failing hadn't kept him from working all his life in television. When he needed help with his writing, the station sent out a secretary to clean up what Dad wrote. So what was the big deal?

As hard as he tried, though, Walt couldn't seem to build up a good head of resentment over the demand that he improve his English. Even *he* knew, when he thought about it, that his weakness in this area wasn't the real reason he refused to keep a journal. The real reason was that the very idea of a journal threatened his sense of privacy.

Mr. Gaetano had said that no one had to write

101

down his deepest secrets. But it was hard to write in a journal without revealing something about yourself. And Walt was of no mind to reveal his personal thoughts to anyone.

As far as Walt was concerned, he had good reason to be touchy. All his life, he'd been in the spotlight. Practically his first memories were of running across the living room in front of the TV lights and sitting on his mother's lap, while she introduced him to the audience of the Manners' breakfast talk show.

All the time he was growing up, his parents had used his most personal problems as material for the discussion segment of their show. If Walt wet the bed, his Mom and Dad would be sure to do a segment on bed-wetting and discuss his habit in detail with some psychologist they'd invited to join them on the air as an expert guest. Later, when Walt had problems adjusting to school, these too had been hashed over at length for the local TV audience. And the same for his first crush on a girl, which became the basis for a cute, nostalgic segment that drew scores of letters of praise from adult viewers — but made the object of Walt's crush so embarrassed at having her name mentioned on the air that she didn't speak to him for months.

After that episode, Walt had finally learned his lesson. Practically growing up on TV had made him a confident performer, who knew how to make himself the center of attention and enjoy every minute of it. But he kept his deeper feelings to himself. Walt Manners had plenty of good pals, but not a single deep friendship. The girls he'd dated all agreed that Walt was a cute guy and lots of fun to be with, but looking back on their dates with Walt, not a one could honestly say that she knew Walt any better when the relationship ended than she had when it began.

Walt's strategy for surviving at Tarenton High had been so successful that he was reluctant to do anything that might change his luck. "Try writing about your own life, a kind of autobiography," Mr. Gaetano had suggested the first day he handed out the journals. But the very idea of writing about Walt Manners made Walt break out in a cold sweat. On paper, the happy-go-lucky person he pretended to be would surely be exposed as a fake.

It only made matters worse that the people he wanted most to like him had taken sides against him from the beginning. Nancy Goldstein, for one, was the kind of girl that Walt secretly admired, even though he probably would never ask her out. Nancy worked hard for what she got, not just in school but at making friends, too. Although the parties she gave always seemed relaxed and spontaneous, Walt knew that it took initiative to bring people together and hard work to make any party a success.

Nevertheless, Walt knew that very few of the kids at school saw this side of Nancy's personality. To most of them, she was a cute kid to whom everything came easy. Just because she was good looking and always wore the best clothes money could buy, it seldom occurred to anyone that Nancy had to try as hard as anyone else to get what she wanted.

Then there was Angie Poletti. If there was one person in the world that Walt had felt he could count on to be more than just a pal, it was Angie. Not that he'd ever tested their friendship, but he'd always felt that in a tight spot Angie would be the one to stick by him.

As Walt worked away at turning his pile of logs into fodder for the wood stove, he'd managed to work up a first-class case of resentment against Angie. By the time he'd finished stacking the wood in the shed at the rear of the house, however, he'd begun to have second thoughts. Angie could hardly help the fact that Tom Gaetano was her cousin, could she? Maybe he'd been too quick to assume that she was unsympathetic.

After finishing his chore, Walt poured himself a Coke and went to his room over the studio. The more he thought about it, the more he liked the idea of giving Angie a call. With any luck, he'd catch her in a mood to listen to his side of the story.

Angie Poletti really was happy when she picked up the telephone and heard Walt's voice on the other end of the line.

"I've been worrying about you all weekend," she told Walt honestly.

"Gee, that's nice to hear," Walt said, flattered.

Now that Walt had reached Angie and found her still willing to talk to him, he wasn't sure where to go with the conversation. For a few minutes, they chatted on about the routines they were preparing for the play-off game.

It was Angie who finally worked the discussion back around to the subject that was on both of their minds. "We really need you on the squad, Walt," she said. "Male cheerleading at Tarenton is your project. I can't imagine what the squad would be like without you."

Walt would rather Angie had worried about him as a person. What if he weren't a cheerleader? Would anyone in the whole world care if he flunked English?

"Why don't you just write something in that stupid journal?" Angie suggested, unaware of Walt's train of thought. "Write anything. Whatever your reasons are for going on strike, they can't be more important than passing English."

Walt was beginning to feel very defensive. What did Angie know about how important his reasons were? She'd never even asked him what they were.

"It's no big deal," he said, resorting to one of his favorite all-purpose expressions. "I do all my other classwork, don't I? I can't believe Gaetano would flunk me over just this one assignment."

"Believe it," Angie warned. "I talked to Tom just last night and he explained his side of the story to me. He didn't want to start a war over this, but if he doesn't keep his word and make the journal a requirement for passing English, he's afraid he'll never be able to make an assignment stick again."

"You talked to Gaetano about me? Good old cousin Tom! I can just see you hashing over my situation behind my back."

For Walt, who was feeling friendless to begin with, Angie's casual admission was the last straw. He'd been betrayed!

Angie, on her part, couldn't quite see why Walt was reacting this way. She'd only been trying to help. Why should she be made to feel guilty?

Like most people secretly afraid to admit any weakness in themselves, Walt vaguely understood that Angie's sympathy was there waiting for him. But to get it, he'd have to ask for it. Or at least show that he was ready to meet her halfway in the discussion. And asking for help of any kind was not something Walt knew how to do.

Instead, he retreated into his shell. "Anyway, I'm glad I called," he groused. "At least now I know for sure whose side you're on."

"Oh, Walt!" Angie groaned. "It's got nothing to do with sides."

"It sure does!" Walt countered.

Angie was losing patience. "Okay, you win," she agreed. "If you want to think that the whole world's against you, then go right ahead. There's no way I can change your mind."

Angie couldn't recall a single time in her whole life that she had ever slammed the phone down in the middle of a conversation. But this time she did.

Walt could hardly believe Angie's reaction. Suddenly the security of his own bedroom, with its carefully framed collection of theater posters, his professional quality stereo system — bought at a discount from one of his parents' DJ friends — began to feel like a prison. He couldn't wait to get back outside.

Grabbing his down jacket and the keys to his jeep, Walt headed out to the garage. When moods like this one hit him, the only cure he knew was to go for a long hike in the woods, and then maybe an even longer drive through country roads that snaked through the hills outside Tarenton. Eventually, he'd calm down enough to think straight. Maybe he'd even figure a way out of his dilemma.

While Walt had been out chopping wood, Olivia Evans had spent her Saturday morning at the Pineland Mall, looking for a new winter coat. Since her mother had insisted on coming with her, the chances of the expedition ending successfully didn't seem promising.

At the moment, Mrs. Evans was standing in front of a store mannequin that happened to be showing a coat Olivia would have given her eye teeth for. It was a trim, two-thirds length coat with padded shoulders that created a silhouette like an inverted triangle. The material was a nubby wool in starkly contrasting colors — black and a vivid purple.

"Looks like something an invader from outer space would wear," Mrs. Evans sniffed.

"I think it's great!" Olivia disagreed.

Olivia knew that she had no hope of ever

looking as sophisticated as tall, slender, Mary Ellen Kirkwood. But her short, wiry figure was suited to the new wave-influenced styles that were in fashion. In fact, Olivia's pale skin, dark eyes, and thick eyebrows, which gave her face a dramatic look even without makeup, were right in vogue. If only she could win a little cooperation from her mother, she would have been able to make the most of her natural assets.

"I know it might seem a little extreme to you," Olivia agreed, trying to be tactful, "but I'm the one that has to wear it."

"And *I'm* the one who has to look out for your interests," Mrs. Evans shot back. "For one thing, that coat is much too short for a cold winter's day. You'd catch the flu the first time you wore it."

"I would not. I'm as healthy as a horse and you know it," Olivia argued back.

Of course, it was useless to try to convince Mrs. Evans of that. Olivia's childhood operations had been a scare that she might be able to put behind her, but her mother would never get over the trauma. In her mind, her little girl would always be a delicate, semi-invalid. And protecting Olivia's health had become an excuse for protecting her daughter from just about every aspect of growing up.

Knowing that she and her mother would never agree on a coat that day, Olivia left Mrs. Evans to select a coat for herself, and drifted across the floor to check out a display of leather handbags in bright hues of red, plum, and sea blue. Although there was no way that a blue handbag could possibly be bad for her health, Olivia felt sure that her mom would think of some reason why it might be. Any style that was not one hundred per cent conservative rated as dangerous in Mrs. Evans' book.

"I hope you're not planning to buy *that* one," a voice behind Olivia said. "Because I just did. We don't want to look like twins."

Olivia turned around and saw that Vanessa Barlow was carrying a bag identical to the one she'd been looking at.

"Don't worry," she said. "I was just window shopping."

"I figured as much. Vanessa studied Olivia's appearance critically. "I mean, that handbag wouldn't exactly go with the rest of your wardrobe. It isn't brown or gray."

Count on Vanessa to turn every conversation into a dig, Olivia thought.

"That's right," Olivia agreed, with mock modesty. "That bag is a little too tacky for me. It is more your speed, Vanessa."

Vanessa tossed her long hair to one side, managing to attract attention from all over the handbags deparment. "Really!" Vanessa said, her voice dripping with condescension. "Why take your disappointment out on me? Just because things haven't worked out between you and Jimmy."

"I don't know what you're talking about," Olivia replied. She wanted to walk away, but her legs felt as if they had turned to jelly. Whatever bad news Vanessa had to deliver, she couldn't resist staying around to hear it.

"Oops! I guess I spoke too soon." Vanessa's attempt to pretend to be sorry didn't have a hint of sincerity. "I just couldn't help thinking that you must be out of the picture. Now that Nancy Goldstein is in it, that is."

"Well, you're wrong." Olivia hoped she sounded more confident about that than she felt.

"Do you mean to tell me that you and Jimmy are *still* going to the dance together?"

"Of course we are."

"Amazing!" Vanessa tossed her head again, a gesture that never failed to show off her cascade of dark hair. "It must be really tough trying to compete with Nancy," she added in feigned sympathy. "After all, she's so much more sophisticated. Especially when it comes to sex."

With that parting shot, Vanessa walked away. Olivia watched her go, feeling that Vanessa had at least cured her of the unrealistic desire to spend forty dollars on a bag she didn't really need. And a handbag wouldn't make her sexy, anyway.

But Vanessa's comparison of her and Nancy had hit home. No doubt about it, Vanessa had meant that Jimmy's interest in Nancy was based on Nancy's willingness to go a lot farther sexually than she was. How could Vanessa know a thing like that? Olivia thought suspiciously. Obviously, she couldn't. But that didn't mean that Vanessa hadn't guessed correctly.

For the rest of the shopping trip, Olivia felt

even more impatient than usual with her mother's attempts to steer her in the direction of the kind of clothes she associated with Girl Scouts and sensible, middle-aged ladies.

Maybe Vanessa was right, she told herself. She, Olivia Evans, was a case of retarded development in every department. Especially sex. Her only chance of proving otherwise was to make sure that Nancy didn't get away with stealing Jimmy right out from under her nose.

CHAPTER

"It's a beautiful clear Saturday here in the vicinity of Narrow Brook Lake. But tonight the temperature should plunge down into the teens. So all you music lovers take my advice: Make sure you have your honey by your side to keep you warm."

Pres flicked off his car radio in disgust. Not only was he not going to have his honey by his side tonight, he wasn't sure if he ever would again. Ever since Kerry Elliot's run-in with his mother, he hadn't so much as talked to her. The reason was simple, too. Fear. Until Kerry came along, it had never occurred to Pres that one reason for his great confidence with women was that he had never cared too deeply what a particular girl thought of him. Now, for the first time in his life, he knew what it was like to be tied up in knots, wondering if a girl still cared for him. He was so

112

afraid of finding out bad news, that it was almost easier to go on avoiding Kerry forever.

In the meantime, Pres had to do something to fill up his spare time, so he was concentrating on his second love — the red Porsche that had been his sixteenth birthday present from his folks. Pulling to a stop in the Keen-way parking lot, Pres left his car and made his way through the acres of groceries to the auto parts center at the rear of the market.

He had completed his errand and was returning by way of the delicious-smelling bakery department when he ran into Angie.

"Pres! Don't tell me you're shopping for groceries!" Angie exclaimed. "I can't believe it!"

"No way." Pres held up his only purchase, a can of winter-weight motor oil. "The only work I do is on my car. Otherwise, I'm totally useless to society."

Angie laughed. There were times when she was tempted to let herself be jealous of Pres for having such an easy life. But how could you resent anyone who was so totally honest about his own laziness? Would you ever know, either, just by looking at Pres, that he was the only son of the richest family in town? As usual, he was wearing jeans and a flannel shirt that had probably cost a bundle when it was originally ordered from some fancy sporting goods store in New York or Chicago. But that had been at least twenty years ago — not in Pres's lifetime. No one else that Angie knew would have worn their parents' hand-me-down clothes by choice.

"Guess who I saw today?" Angie said, as if she were bringing up the subject by the merest chance. "Kerry Elliot. She was walking her dog in the park."

"Kerry! How is she? Did she say anything about me?" His eagerness was so obvious.

Pres's response made Angie realize that he must be in a bad way. The old, casual Pres she had known most of her life would never have let it show that he cared about a girl.

"She's okay," Angie said. "But I think she's wondering why you haven't called or spoken to her for days."

Pres looked abashed. "Too embarrassed, I guess. Did she mention what happened up at my house the other day?"

"Just that your mom hadn't made her feel too welcome." Angie didn't want Pres to think that she had been gossiping with Kerry about his family, so she pretended ignorance of the details.

Pres wasn't fooled. "That's all right. I don't mind Kerry's telling you. But keep the story quiet, okay? My mother usually isn't like that. It's just that she's been unhappy lately. I think that she and my father might be having some problems."

"That's too bad," Angie commiserated.

"I don't know exactly what's wrong," Pres said. "I wish Mom had someone she could talk things over with."

"What about you?" Angie asked.

Pres looked surprised. "What do you mean?"

"I mean," Angie said, "why don't *you* talk to her? Or won't she discuss it with you?"

"To tell you the truth, I haven't had a chance. Mom's been avoiding me lately, especially since her scene with Kerry. She spends a lot of time in her room with a 'Do Not Disturb' sign on the door. And when we are together, usually the maid is there, so we can't really talk."

Angie was beginning to get the picture that Pres's home life did not remotely resemble her own.

"Well, I think you should at least let her know that you're worried about her," she said lamely. "In the meantime, what about Kerry? Aren't you going to call her? She cares about you Pres . . . and she's so sweet and vulnerable."

"I guess I will," Pres said thoughtfully, "if you think she'll be willing to talk to me."

"I know she will," Angie said.

"It's weird," Pres thought out loud. "I would have guessed that you'd be the last person to want to smooth things over between me and Kerry. Considering that she used to be Andrew's girl."

"I know," Angie admitted. "But seeing how upset Kerry was made me realize that what happened was no one's fault. Even Andrew doesn't think so anymore, so why should I?"

Pres looked relieved. "It's good to hear that at least *one* member of the squad isn't angry with me. What with my little run-in with Walt and my own worries, I haven't been much use at practice lately."

"Walt's been acting really strange, too," Angie said. "I just had the weirdest conversation with him on the phone. I only wanted to help, and somehow I ended up being the villain in his eyes."

"Yeah," Pres agreed. "I don't try to figure Walt out. He's too deep for me."

"*Walt? Deep?*" Angie practically choked on the words. "Walt's the last person I would call deep."

Pres understood Angie's reaction. But he'd always felt that Walt had a hidden side to his personality. "It's just a thought," Pres said, feeling unwilling to dissect Walt. "Anyway, I'd be the last one to ever figure out exactly what Walt's problem is. I'd be happy if I could just manage to remember that routine he was trying to show us the other day. There's no reason why the whole squad should make fools of ourselves next Friday, just because we've having our differences."

"I agree with you there." Angie was struck by a sudden inspiration. "Are you doing anything special this afternoon?"

"Me?" Pres held up his can of oil again. "I was just planning to spend the afternoon tinkering with the car. Not that there's anything that really needs doing. It's just my way of wasting time."

"Why don't you come over to my house and we can go over some of our routines on our own. I'll call Mom and tell her she doesn't need to pick me up here. We can both use the extra practice, and at least it would be a way of showing Walt

116

that we *do* care about making his idea look good."

"What about Andrew?" Pres frowned. "I'm not sure I'm ready to run into him."

"That's okay," Angie assured him. "Andrew's spending the day at a friend's house and staying overnight. He won't be around."

"Then you're on."

They were out in the parking lot, trying to figure out a way to stuff Angie's three bags of groceries into the tiny luggage space of the Porsche when Nancy Goldstein came by with Sue Yardley and two other girl friends.

"I don't think that car is exactly made for practical errands," Nancy giggled.

"That's never been a problem up until now. There's never been even *one* bag of groceries in it," Pres said as he frantically repacked one of the bags so that it would fit into the narrow space behind the driver's seat.

"So what's up?" Nancy's first thought was that Pres and Angie were planning a party of some sort and hadn't invited her. A quick inspection of the contents of the grocery bags made that thought seem doubtful — unless cornflakes and detergent were the new "in" thing to serve at parties.

Angie quickly explained that she and Pres were headed to her place for an impromptu practice session. "Want to come along?" she added.

"Sounds like a great idea. I sure didn't get much accomplished yesterday," Nancy admitted. "My body felt like a disaster area after skiing. I could use a good workout to get rid of the kinks." She glanced questioningly at Sue and the other two girls she'd come with, all of whom indicated that they wouldn't feel deserted if Nancy took up the invitation.

"I'd love to come along," she said finally. "But is there room?"

"Sure," Angie said. "You can sit on my lap. There's plenty of room."

Pres rolled his eyes in mock distress. "My poor car. It's never had to work this hard."

"Don't be silly," Angie laughed. "What's a car for if you can't use it for practical things?"

Nancy could hardly keep from grinning ear to ear, as she carefully lowered herself into the tiny space between Angie's lap and the dashboard. It was just like Angie to be oblivious to the difference in glamor quotient between a Porsche and, say, a Dodge sedan.

Once Nancy was settled in, Pres headed out onto the road, driving with extra care to avoid sudden stops.

"I think my foot is already developing a case of pins and needles," Angie observed cheerfully after a few blocks. "But I guess it's worth it. I just hope Walt Manners will appreciate the sacrifices we're making here so that his new routine looks good on Friday night."

But Walt was in no mood to be appreciative. Finishing a brisk hike along one of the trails that followed the undeveloped side of Narrow

Brook Lake, Walt had driven his jeep aimlessly for nearly an hour, trying to make up his mind how to spend the rest of his Saturday. He had just decided to stop by the Pinelands Mall in hopes of finding some kids from school to hang around with, when he spotted Pres's red car on the road with Angie and Nancy crammed like a pair of sardines into the passenger seat.

What's going on? Walt muttered to himself.

A look at the grocery bags stuffed behind the car's seats suggested one explanation, the same one that had occurred to Nancy minutes earlier: Some sort of party was in the works, and Walt hadn't been invited.

If the Porsche hadn't made a right turn onto Crossways Road, Walt would no doubt have pulled even with Pres's car at the stoplight and gotten an explanation. As it was, he couldn't resist following the Porsche to see where the group was headed. After several blocks on Crossways, when the Porsche turned off onto Elm Drive, Walt was pretty sure that Pres and company were going to Angie Poletti's place.

Suddenly, the resentment that he had spent most of the afternoon trying to reason himself out of was back in full force. He had just talked to Angie a few hours ago and she hadn't mentioned anything about a get together at her place. And why was the squad, or at least 50% of it, meeting without him? Angie had seemed awfully sure that his battle with Mr. Gaetano was going to end with him flunking English and getting bounced from the squad. Maybe the squad had decided not to wait for the inevitable. Maybe they were already taking it for granted that Walt was on his way out.

The last thing he was in the mood for right now was to confront Angie, Pres, and Nancy all at once. Instinctively, he dropped back into the line of traffic hoping that Pres wouldn't notice his all too conspicuous black Cherokee jeep. At the next light, he turned off to the right and headed along a roundabout route of back streets that he judged would bring him around past the Poletti house just about the time the others arrived from the opposite direction.

As bothered as he was by the suspicion that Pres, Angie, and Nancy were meeting behind his back, Walt was not too depressed to enjoy the fantasy of himself as a private eye, tailing a car full of suspects. In his daydream, moon-faced, stocky Walt Manners — the eternal joker who was always in hot water over some prank or another — was instantly replaced by his alter ego: Walt Manners, secret agent. This imaginary Walt was an ace spy who combined the suave good looks of Remington Steele with the macho ruggedness of Lee Majors.

The transformation felt terrific! Walt hunched over the steering wheel of the jeep, picturing how surprised Pres and company would be when Walt just happened to drive by and give them all an unconcerned wave, just as they were heading into Angie's house for their secret meeting. He would pretend total indifference, of course. But it would be a way of serving notice that you couldn't pull a fast one on Walt Manners.

By now, Walt had swung onto Henley Street, which ran parallel to the road where Angie's house stood. At each corner he peered up the side street to the right, checking to make sure that the Porsche hadn't picked up speed. By his calculation there should be just enough time for him to circle around and pass Angie's place in the opposite direction as the Porsche pulled into her driveway. The timing was critical, but Walt felt sure that he had figured out the maneuver perfectly.

Bang! The sound of his front bumper slamming into the rear of another vehicle jarred Walt out of his fantasy world instantly. Lost in his daydream and with his eyes glued to the side street, he hadn't noticed that the car ahead of him had not yet pulled through the stop sign. Fortunately, the jeep had only been going between five and ten miles an hour, but the impact was enough to shatter the right taillight of the car and give its occupants a good jolt.

There goes my perfect driving record, Walt thought automatically. Television private eyes never seemed to have to worry about little details like insurance. Not to mention the problem of how to break the bad news to their parents.

This automatic reaction was soon replaced by another — fear. What if someone in the other car had been hurt?

Leaping out of the jeep, Walt ran to the driver's

side of the other car, his face a mask of worry. "Are you all right?" he gasped.

"No thanks to you."

The familiar voice registered on Walt's consciousness, before he'd had a chance to recognize the driver.

"Why don't you watch where you're going?" the voice went on. "A car isn't some kind of toy. I've got my two daughters in here. They could have been hurt."

Walt listened with his heart sagging to his shoes as Mr. Gaetano let off steam. This time, Walt had no clever comeback to make. Gaetano's anger was all too justified.

Walt had always been quite proud of his driving ability. Now, he felt shaken to realize the mess he'd made by taking his eye off the road for a few seconds. What if there had been a bicycle on the road instead of a good-sized sedan? Or even a pedestrian? He could have caused a really serious accident.

"Look, I'm sorry. I really am," he apologized, when Mr. Gaetano had come to the end of his lecture.

"Good," Gaetano said, calming down considerably. "I just hope you've learned a lesson from this." Walking around to the back of his car, he examined the shattered taillight critically. "It could be worse, I suppose."

After a few minutes of discussion, the two agreed that Harry's Garage in town could look over the Gaetano car. If nothing was broken except the taillight, which seemed to be the case, Walt would pay the damage out of his own pocket. Fortunately, he had some money in his savings account left over from his summer job. It would be a lot easier that way than getting the insurance company involved, which was sure to set his parents on the warpath.

Walt followed the Gaetano car to Harry's, where it took fifteen minutes or so for a mechanic to look over the car and decide that there was no serious damage. Luckily, too, the garage was able to lend the Gaetano family a car so that they could do the repair work over the weekend.

By the time Walt left the garage and headed for home, he had decided privately that Tom Gaetano might not be such a bad guy after all. A lot of people would have been a lot less reasonable than Gaetano had been, particularly when the other driver was a teenager. More amazing still, Gaetano hadn't even referred to their problems in class, even though he had every reason to be fed up with Walt. For the first time since the battle over the journal started, Walt felt a twinge of guilt. Maybe he should have given the new English teacher a break after all.

As for the gathering at Angie's house, Walt was already beginning to lose interest. Even though he was still none too happy at the thought of being excluded, he had decided that his plan to make Angie, Pres, and Nancy feel guilty had been pretty silly from the beginning. If they hadn't cared enough to invite him in the first place, why should they feel guilty if he happened to drive past and catch them in the act? They probably wouldn't have even cared if they realized that Walt knew all about their little Saturday afternoon meeting.

Deciding to chalk up the whole afternoon's mess to experience, Walt headed on home.

CHAPTER

Vanessa Barlow had enjoyed a very successful Saturday.

By four o'clock in the afternoon she was headed home from the shopping mall, the backseat of her mother's car piled high with purchases. The total bill for her day's amusement had come to just over two hundred dollars — a bit breathtaking even by Vanessa's standards — but she was quite pleased with the way she'd managed to spread the damage over five different credit cards belonging to her mother.

Experience had taught Vanessa that credit card debts never seemed to affect her mother the way the news of cash outlays did. The bills didn't arrive for over a month, and then they trickled in one by one. By that time Vanessa had usually managed to figure out ways to convince Mrs. Barlow that at least some of her purchases had been dire necessities. And a certain percentage of the bills were never connected to Vanessa at all. An impulse shopper herself, Mrs. Barlow could never be absolutely certain that the forty dollars spent in Marnie's sportswear department in a given month hadn't been for some forgotten purchase of her own. Vanessa, of course, usually did her best to convince her mother that this had indeed been the case.

On this particular day, Vanessa was just a little worried that she might attract attention while sneaking her shopping bags up to her room. Just to play it safe, she'd decided to put some gas in her mother's car before returning it. That way, her mom might not even notice that Vanessa had been out in the car all day. And if she did see Vanessa coming home, at least Vanessa could score a few brownie points by bragging that she had actually replaced the gas she'd used.

Pulling into the full-service lane at Harry's, Vanessa automatically checked herself out in the mirror before ordering five dollars worth of premium.

"Sure you don't want me to fill it up?" the gas jockey asked.

"Are you kidding?" Vanessa looked at him as if he'd taken leave of his senses. "It isn't *my* car."

"I get it. Wouldn't want to give your folks a heart attack." The attendant, whose name was Duane Richards, chuckled at his own joke.

Vanessa ignored him. Although she'd been coming to Harry's ever since she got her license and Duane had always been friendly, she considered him beneath her notice.

Normally, everything that happened at Harry's was beneath Vanessa's notice. But today, as she gazed around while waiting for the gas, she saw something rather interesting.

"Doesn't that sedan over there belong to Mr. Gaetano?" she asked idly. "You know, the man who teaches at Tarenton High."

"That's right," Duane agreed. "Had a little fender bender. Just happened about an hour ago."

"Really! I hope no one was hurt."

"No one hurt at all. They were all in here getting an estimate. You just missed them."

"All? Oh. You mean the other driver? And who was that?" Vanessa's curiosity was always insatiable.

Duane was quite pleased to be making small talk with the very attractive Vanessa. If he noticed that he was being pumped for information, he didn't seem to mind.

"You know Walt Manners," he said. "He must be in your class at school. Ran right into the back of Gaetano's car down on Henley Street."

The gears inside Vanessa's head were already spinning, putting the scene together. "I bet his goose is cooked for sure," she thought out loud.

"Oh no, I don't think so." Duane disagreed. "I've known Tom Gaetano since he was a kid. He has a temper, but he isn't one to hold a grudge in the long run."

This last bit of news didn't particularly please Vanessa. She had rather been looking forward to seeing Walt's problems with Gaetano escalate to the point where he'd have to give up cheerleading. She had even begun to think that there might be an opportunity shaping up for her to make the squad after all. Naturally, Ardith Engborg *would* want to replace Walt with another guy. But who?

Most of the guys in school who were athletic enough for cheerleading had already gone out for a sport. Of the rest, Vanessa couldn't think of a single guy who combined the outgoing personality of a cheerleader with enough interest in the squad to make all those practice sessions worthwhile. And knowing Ardith, she'd restructure the entire squad before she'd consider taking on a cheerleader who was second best, male or female.

So far, Walt had been doing a great job of making trouble for himself. From Vanessa's point of view, it seemed unfair that the situation might resolve itself without benefitting *her*.

Following that line of reasoning to its natural conclusion, Vanessa decided that she would be justified in helping things along. The plan was already formulating in her mind. It was going to be so easy that Vanessa couldn't help feeling rather pleased with herself.

Walt Manners was in the studio, where his parents stored the equipment used for their broadcasts from the house. The accident momentarily forgotten, he was hard at work putting together a tape of dance music that he had thought of using for a squad routine. Since the school band didn't play at basketball games, the squad used recorded music, at least before the game when the crowd was waiting for the action to get underway.

Walt knew he'd have his hands full selling the new routine to Ardith and the other members of the squad, but he was used to that. Compared to putting male cheerleaders on the squad in the first place, his routines would be a minor departure from tradition.

Walt's ideas for the squad were always more theatrical than anyone else's, and he had to admit to himself that for him cheerleading would always be a substitute for dancing and acting, two activities that there weren't a whole lot of chances to pursue in Tarenton. Most likely, he'd never get the chance to pursue them fulltime anywhere. His chunky body was not what most choreographers looked for in a dancer, and his round, cheerful face would never qualify him as a leading man. No doubt he'd end up like his father, who had given up a stalled career in acting to become a local TV emcee and "personality." Or else, he'd drift into some form of behind-the-scenes work in the theater or broadcasting. That wouldn't be so bad, really, but for the moment Walt was enjoying his chance to be on center stage as a varsity cheerleader.

He enjoyed it so much that he knew he'd eventually have to find a way to pass English — even if that meant giving in and writing in that journal. Although he hadn't thought it through, his decision was already half made. All he needed was a graceful way of giving in.

Walt had just finished splicing the last song onto his master tape when the ringing of the phone sent him sprinting into the kitchen. "Hi!"

said a honeyed voice on the other end of the line. "It's me. Vanessa."

Walt frowned. There was nothing routine about Vanessa calling him at home at six o'clock on a Saturday night. Something was definitely up. But what?

"I just heard about your accident," Vanessa purred, "and I want you to know that I, for one, intend to stand by you. No matter *what*."

Walt glared at the phone. "How could you know about that? It just happened."

Vanessa was glad he'd asked. So far, her script was unfolding according to plan. "Well, you know how it is," she said evasively. "When your father is the school superintendent, you hear things."

Just as Vanessa had hoped, Walt jumped to the obvious conclusion. "But how could your old man know? Did someone tell him?"

Of course, Vanessa had never quite said her father did know. Could she help it if Walt read too much into her words? "I don't want to say too much," she went on. "I could get in trouble." All of which was only too true.

Then she added her parting shot. "They say Mr. Gaetano has a reputation for having a short fuse."

"That snake! I can't believe it." Walt was totally indignant. "He promised he wouldn't make a big issue of the accident, and not two hours later he's already complained about me to the superintendent of schools. And why? Don't tell me he's trying to claim that what happened had something to do with our not getting along in class!"

Until that moment, it hadn't occurred to Walt that such a claim would be all too easy to make. After all, he'd run into the Gaetano car from behind, when it was stopped for a stop sign.

Vanessa was so pleased with her success that she had to bite her lower lip to keep from laughing out loud. "Well, *I* will never believe that it was anything but an accident," she said.

"But it *wasn't* anything but an accident," Walt protested.

"Uh oh. I gotta go now. My dad just came in," Vanessa replied. And she hung up, just in time to keep Walt from hearing the bursts of laughter she could no longer hold inside.

Walt, for his part, was in no mood for humor. He'd been more or less resigned to going to see Gaetano on Monday morning to find out how he could make up the days he'd missed doing his journal assignment. Now he just couldn't see doing any such thing.

As one who'd been a few steps ahead of disaster before in his school career, Walt knew that there was no point in apologizing before he knew exactly what the charges against him were going to be. Until he found out, he'd just keep on as before.

CHAPTER

12

Vanessa was not the only one in Tarenton who was busy on he phone that weekend.

Pres had finally gotten up the nerve to call Kerry.

"I had a long talk with my mom today," Pres was saying. "She's really sorry if she upset you."

"I couldn't stand what she said about me, Pres," Kerry said. "She made me feel as if I was just another girl in a long line of Pres Tilford conquests."

Pres gripped the phone tighter. "That's not true, Kerry. You're special to me. You have to believe that. I've had a lot of girls, I admit it. But I've never really cared about one of them. Not like you."

"I don't know, Pres. I feel out of your league. Maybe we should just —"

"Mom didn't have anything against you personally," Pres interrupted. "She said that sometimes she's actually jealous of all the girls I go out with, because they get more attention than she gets from Dad. Anyway, she and Dad are trying to work things out. Things will be better from now on."

"That's great." Kerry said wearily. "I'm happy that everything is better for you. Really."

"What about you and me?" Pres asked softly. "You aren't angry are you? Will you come to the dance with me after Friday's game?"

Kerry hesitated. "No to the first question. I'm not angry. I don't know about the second part. Maybe we shouldn't go out anymore."

Pres felt his heart drop. He needed Kerry. "But why?" he sputtered. "Unless you really are angry."

"It's hard to explain." Kerry said. "But I guess I know what your mom means about being jealous."

Women! Pres thought. "How can you be jealous when I can't get you out of my mind? You don't think I'm fooling around with anybody else, do you? I can tell you I'm not."

"Not now," Kerry admitted. "But in a couple of days, or a couple of weeks, maybe, you will be. I haven't been walking around Tarenton with blinders on all these years. Just about the time I'm really hooked, when I've let myself fall in love with you, you'll lose interest. And I'll be left to drive myself crazy wanting you."

Pres was dumbstruck. No girl he could remember had ever raised this objection before. And now, when for once he had found someone he wanted to love forever, his past was coming back to haunt him.

"Trust me, Kerry." As soon as the words were out of his mouth, Pres knew they wouldn't be enough. He'd said that to at least two dozen girls in the past year. Even to him, it was starting to sound like a line.

The best Pres could do was to get Kerry to promise not to make a decision right away. He'd wait until Friday if necessary. He certainly didn't want to go to the dance with any other girl.

At the other end of town, Mary Ellen had been daydreaming about Patrick.

On Sunday morning, she'd awakened early, clutching her pillow for dear life. The heat was already on in the house, and she'd been dreaming that it was summer and she was at the Narrow Brook Lake public beach. She'd been stretched out on the sand with the dreamiest guy in the world beside her. At first, she hadn't been able to see his face. She'd been gently rubbing suntan oil onto his chest and muscular back. Then she'd decided that what she really wanted to be doing was kissing him.

It was only after the endless dream kiss was finished that she'd suddenly been able to see the face of her companion.

Patrick!

As soon as she'd recognized him, Patrick had started to dissolve. Although she tried to grab him and hold on as tight as she could, the dream Patrick slowly but surely slipped away from her.

She was left wide awake, clinging to her pillow.

Mary Ellen didn't need a psychiatrist to tell her what the dream meant. She'd known all along that Patrick was the one guy who really turned her on. That was exactly the problem!

If she and Patrick ever became a couple, it would be only a matter of time until they were sleeping together. There would be no half-way relationship for them. Then, knowing Patrick, he would want to get engaged. To get married, even.

What scared Mary Ellen was that she might want that, too. If she couldn't forget Patrick now, how would she ever manage to break off with him once they were lovers? And if she couldn't, all her dreams of a modeling career and a life in New York would go right down the drain.

Mary Ellen had been through this a hundred times before. This time, however, she was coming to a different conclusion. Why should she turn her back on love just because of something that might happen months from now? Or years? She'd make those decisions about the future when the time came.

It took half a dozen tries before she got hold of Patrick, who had been out helping his father repair the Henley Trash truck. By then, Mary Ellen had rehearsed what she wanted to say so many times that she couldn't possibly back down.

"I was thinking about our conversation a few days ago," she began. "The one after cheerleading practice. And I've decided to declare an end to the ice age."

"Terrific!" Patrick yelled.

Mary Ellen waited for the expected followup. "So," she said at last, "how about celebrating by inviting me to be your date for the dance Friday night?"

Patrick was silent and then he said slowly, "I'd love to —"

"Good —"

"The thing is," Patrick interrupted her, "I can't. I've already got a date."

"You do! Who with?"

"Vanessa Barlow, actually." Patrick sounded sheepish, not a usual mood for him. "I guess I just sort of fell into it."

"I bet you did!" Mary Ellen was choking with anger and humiliation. "Well, when you manage to claw your way out of whatever you 'just fell into' don't call me." She slammed down the phone.

It took several hours before she was ready to admit that she was really angrier with herself than with Patrick. She'd played hard to get for too long. And now. . . .

No sooner was the thought formed, though, than she changed her mind. Her reasons for resisting Patrick had never been a game. They were very important to her. How could he have hung around for so long, pleading with her to change her mind about him, only to dump her for Vanessa?

That was the end. The ultimate betrayal.

Mary Ellen snatched the pillow from her bed and pounded it with her fists. If that pillow really had been Patrick in the flesh, he would have been black and blue for a week.

Of all the kids who were having problems with dates for Friday's dance, Jimmy Hilbert was unique. Nancy and Olivia were both under the impression that they were going to be his date that night.

Not that Jimmy had a guilty conscience. For one thing, Jimmy's conscience was the only muscle in his body that he never exercised. For another, he was too carried away with congratulating himself for having two girls fighting over him.

In Jimmy's mind, the solution to the problem was simple. Two girls were competing. All he had to do was make up his mind who the lucky winner was going to be. Fortunately, he didn't have to think too hard to come up with the perfect test. On Wednesday afternoon, Mr. and Mrs. Hilbert were leaving for a bar association convention in Chicago. They were planning to be gone overnight and were leaving Jimmy to take care of himself and the house. Jimmy was sure he *could,* too.

Thinking it over, Jimmy had decided that Nancy Goldstein was the girl who would be most likely to understand and appreciate the possibilities opened up by his parents' trip. On Sunday night, right after he got the news himself, he dialed Nancy's number.

He started by suggesting that Nancy come over Wednesday night for dinner. "My folks have an electric grill in the kitchen," he said. "I can cook us up some steaks. It'll be great. Just the two of us."

To Nancy, it sounded good. All except the timing. "I'd love to come over," she said, "but I've got cheerleading practice. It's the last one before the Grove Lake game, too. No way I can miss it."

"How about after practice?" Jimmy suggested.

"Okay, but we won't have much time," Nancy said. "My mother will want me home by ten-thirty at the latest."

"I think we can solve that problem." Boldly, Jimmy suggested that Nancy just might tell her mother that she was planning to stay overnight with a girl friend. "That way," he went on, "we could go out to some of the late-night clubs in Grove Lake. I'm sure we'd get in. I've even got some borrowed ID."

"And then what?" Nancy's voice was dripping with suspicion.

Jimmy decided not to push his luck. "That's strictly up to you. You know what *I'd* like," he said softly. "But it's a big house."

"It couldn't be big enough to suit me," Nancy snapped.

Jimmy couldn't believe it. The conversation had been going so well. "Does that mean you won't do it?" he asked.

"That's *exactly* what it means," Nancy shot back. "We've only gone out a few times. And meanwhile, you've been dating Olivia Evans, too.

Don't think I haven't heard about that."

The sound of Nancy slamming the phone down was so loud that Jimmy held the receiver at arm's length. So much for his hunch that Nancy would be a willing date, he told himself. Or maybe not. Maybe he just hadn't been subtle enough. What girl in her right mind would turn down Jimmy Hilbert, if the offer was made in the right way?

As he picked up the phone again to dial Olivia, Jimmy decided that this time he would play it cool. He wouldn't mention his idea about her spending the night. He'd just stick with the invitation to dinner for the time being.

Olivia turned out to be a different kind of surprise. Shy, unsophisticated Olivia — Olivia who had so far been totally untouchable — agreed without an argument to Jimmy's plan for dinner at his house on Wednesday.

Jimmy was so amazed that he was almost, but not quite, suspicious that Olivia had missed his broad hints about the advantages of their having the *whole* house to themselves.

Olivia was if anything even more surprised to hear herself say yes. In fact, if Jimmy hadn't automatically suggested making the date for *after* cheerleading practice, she probably would have agreed to skip practice — something she never did.

Olivia's problem was that she was desperate. Not for Jimmy personally. Not for dates. Or even for male interest in general. She was desperate for a chance to build up her sagging self-confidence.

She was tired of hearing Angie talk about how special Marc's kisses made her feel. She was tired of watching Patrick and Pres and half the guys in school chase after Mary Ellen. She was tired of wondering how she could possibly compete with a sophisticated, sexy-looking girl like Nancy.

Olivia had begun to feel that sexual experience was like a kind of secret club ritual that all her friends knew about except her. Of course, even Angie, who was practically engaged to Marc, said that she would never actually go to bed with him. But Olivia wasn't even sure that this was the truth. For all she knew, everyone did it except her. She and Michael had been so shy that they'd barely gotten to square one, and she was sure her total ignorance must be obvious to the whole world.

Olivia wasn't stupid. She knew that Jimmy's plans for the evening included going beyond the good-night kiss stage. Just how far beyond, she wasn't exactly sure. But at this point anything was better than being a total babe in the woods. She only wished that she could look forward to Wednesday night. She liked Jimmy. At least she'd been telling herself for weeks that this was the next thing to being in love with him. Still, she felt as if their upcoming date was not so much a chance to enjoy each other's company as a kind of club initiation that she would have to grit her teeth and get through, one way or another.

Olivia walked through the first three days of the school week in a numb daze. She barely heard what went on in classes. She jumped and yelled like a robot at cheerleading practice. Luckily, no one noticed. At practice, the whole squad had been on the stiff side. Everyone was still mad at everyone else, but the need to be prepared for Friday's game had triumphed. No one had any good humor left over for kidding around, so Olivia's moodiness didn't attract any attention.

After practice on Wednesday, Olivia spent longer than usual getting dressed. She didn't wear anything special, just slacks and a nice plum-colored sweater. But underneath her sweater she had on a shrimp-colored silk camisole that she'd bought for her cousin's wedding and never worn since. It was the closest thing she owned to sexy lingerie and, best of all, it hid the three vertical scars from her operations. No matter what happened, she was determined not to let Jimmy get a look at those scars.

By the time she was finished making up and went outside to meet Jimmy, she was really nervous. It was the kind of nervousness that always made Olivia talkative and giddy.

"You're in a good mood today," Jimmy said approvingly as he drove. "What happened to quiet, serious Olivia Evans?"

"Oh, I don't know." Olivia laughed. "I guess she isn't here tonight." If she were, Olivia thought silently, she'd be screaming at me to forget this nonsense and go home. The thought made her laugh even more.

At the Hilbert house, Jimmy immediately disappeared into the kitchen. "Wait till you try this," he shouted out to Olivia in the living room. "My folks have a great cellar."

"Cellar?"

"You know. For wine." Jimmy reappeared, carrying a bottle of red wine and two crystal glasses.

Olivia took a tentative sip of the wine Jimmy poured for her, and put the glass down. "I guess I'm not thirsty," she said.

Jimmy howled with laughter. "You don't have to be thirsty to drink wine." And to demonstrate, he finished off his glass in one gulp.

Then, all of a sudden, Jimmy pounced. His mouth clamped onto hers in a clumsy, unappealing kiss. Olivia felt herself pushed backward into the corner of the couch. It was all happening so fast! It didn't take her long to decide that she didn't care for Jimmy's style.

She liked it even less when she felt his hand begin to move under her sweater. She pushed his hand away, but Jimmy was not about to be discouraged.

The sensation of his cold hand on her warm skin jolted Olivia back to the unpleasant reality of the situation she was in. What am I doing here? she thought. I don't really *like* this boy, no less *love* him. I don't have to prove anything to myself *or* him. I am who I am, and it's okay.

Olivia squirmed free, nearly dumping Jimmy on the floor in the process.

Jimmy's face was a mask of surprise. "What's going on?" he gulped.

Olivia reached for the first excuse that came

to mind. "I think I don't feel so good," she said. "Maybe it was that sip of wine."

Just hearing herself say it, Olivia felt stupid. All her life she'd hated it when her mother used her little girl's health as an excuse for why Olivia shouldn't do things. Now she was doing the very same thing. Then and there, Olivia made a decision.

"No. That's not true!" she said. "I'm not sick at all. What I am is mad."

Jimmy, sinking into the depths of the sofa, looked almost funny to her. His sauve macho act interrupted, he had suddenly turned to Jell-O.

"You don't care about me at all," Olivia went on accusingly. "You just wanted to take advantage of your parents being away. Any girl at all would do. All you want is a *body*. You're really a creep."

Olivia didn't wait for an answer. Grabbing her coat and scarf, she stormed out the door of the Hilbert house. She was halfway down the driveway before it occurred to her that she was going to have a very long walk home. But she felt free, as if she had done something important.

CHAPTER

13

For someone who was in deep trouble, Walt was feeling awfully triumphant.

All week long he had been waiting for Mr. Gaetano to show his true colors. Today, when Walt reported for his after school detention it had finally happened.

"On Friday I've got to turn in my preliminary list of students in danger of failing English," Gaetano had explained. "It's up to you, Walt, to decide whether you want to be on it or not. If you want to pass, you'll have to give me your word that you'll make up the journal assignments you've missed so far."

Mr. Gaetano was trying to give Walt one last chance. What Walt heard was a threat. And the phrase "give me your word" struck an especially sour chord.

"*My* word!" Walt said. "What good is a promise to you? You said you wouldn't get me into trouble about the accident. And not an hour later, you'd reported me to the superintendent of schools."

"I have no idea what you're talking about," Mr. Gaetano protested. "I haven't even talked to Dr. Barlow."

"Maybe not. Maybe you reported me to Mrs. Oetjen and she told Barlow. What's the difference? I still can't trust you."

Now that Walt thought he wasn't to blame, failing English no longer seemed so bad. It proved what he'd been feeling. The whole world was against him. His only real friend was himself.

Even though Walt was busy congratulating himself, he was still paying careful attention to the road. The bill for fixing the Gaetano car had been large enough to teach him one lesson at least. He noticed the small, fast-moving form of Olivia Evans as soon as he came over the crest of Robin's Hill. She was just starting up the hill coming toward him, her face already red from the effort.

Walt drove down the hill and came to a stop at Olivia's side. "What are you doing way out here?" he asked.

"What does it look like I'm doing?" Olivia puffed. "Walking."

"Want a ride?"

Olivia shook her head. "No thanks. I'm perfectly capable of taking care of myself."

Walt grinned. "I never said you weren't. That doesn't mean you can't accept a ride, does it?"

Olivia looked longingly at the passenger seat

of the jeep. It was more than three miles to the nearest bus stop. Most of them uphill. And it was already beginning to get dark. "Okay," she agreed. "But don't ask me what I'm doing out here on this road."

"I wouldn't think of it," Walt assured her. But that was one promise no mere human could keep. Less than a mile up the road, his curiosity was already getting the better of him. "I can't help it," he said. "What are you doing out here?"

"You'd never understand," Olivia said, "because you've always been part of the in-crowd. But when you go through life feeling that you have something to prove, you can end up getting into some dumb situations."

Walt winced. Somehow the problem Olivia was describing sounded all too familiar. "Maybe I would understand," he said. "Try me."

Half sputtering with embarrassment and half laughing, Olivia related the story of her wrestling match with Jimmy Hilbert. "At least it was an instant cure for my crush on him," she giggled ruefully. "Jimmy is a jerk. But I hate to think that he'll tell the story all over school and make me look ridiculous."

"I have the idea that he won't do that," Walt said. Only that day after English class, he explained, he'd heard Nancy Goldstein tell Susan that she'd been invited to Jimmy's house that evening and turned him down. "So far Jimmy has been playing the two of you against each other," Walt added, "and it worked like a charm. You were mad at Nancy. Nancy was mad at you. Neither of you was mad at Jimmy. Which you would have been, if you and Nancy had ever thought of talking the situation over with each other."

"I guess you're right," Olivia agreed. "This whole argument never would have gotten started if I'd just trusted my friends on the squad."

As Walt's jeep pulled up in front of the Evans house, Olivia reached over and gave him a big hug. "Thanks for the advice," she said. "I won't forget. Squad loyalty forever!"

Squad loyalty!

That was all very well for Olivia. But Walt still wasn't sure how that motto was supposed to apply to him. He was still wondering where, if anywhere, he fit in.

Walt was almost home when he remembered that his parents were going to be working late at the broadcasting studio that evening. There would be no dinner waiting for him. Turning his jeep around, he headed back toward the Burger King near Pineland Mall and went inside for a hamburger and shake.

The Burger King was almost empty except for one woman who was with her three children at a table in the far corner. Walt took a table at the opposite side of the room and sat down to eat. Although he loved being the center of attention in any group, for some reason he always felt awkward and conspicuous when he had to be in a public place alone. To pass the time, he started watching a blonde girl in a Burger King uniform and hat who was busy cleaning up the mess left by departed patrons.

His hamburger was almost gone before he finally realized who she was. Cindy Hartman from school! Although he'd been in classes with Cindy for years, he'd never really noticed her before — except lately, as Vanessa Barlow's newest shadow.

Cindy's looks made her perfect for that role. She was Vanessa's opposite in almost every way. In fact, if Vanessa were a photograph, Cindy might have been the negative. She had natural white-blonde hair and very pale skin, in contrast to the tawny, dark Vanessa. Her figure was lanky and angular, where Vanessa's was all curves. And she was as quiet as Vanessa was melodramatic.

Noticing her now, Walt couldn't help thinking that Cindy looked interesting. Not pretty maybe, but interesting. It was too bad that she was tied to Vanessa's apron strings.

It was almost as if Cindy was able to read his mind.

Looking up from her work, she smiled shyly in Walt's direction. "Hi," she ventured. "I'm in your class at Tarenton High."

"Of course," Walt grinned. "I know who you are. Cindy Hartman."

Cindy looked pleased. Walt, meanwhile, breathed an invisible sigh of relief that he remembered her name in time. All of his good friends, whatever problems they might have, were class stars. He could hardly imagine what it would be like to think that other kids in his own

148

class might not remember who he was.

"Can I sit down?" Cindy asked nervously. "I think I ought to talk to you."

"Sure." Walt had no idea what was coming.

"I guess I shouldn't tell you this . . . but I've been feeling guilty for days."

"Guilty?" Walt repeated dumbly.

"Yeah. See, I was in the room when Vanessa called you last Saturday. We planned it ahead of time."

"Planned it?"

Cindy laughed. "You're starting to sound like an echo."

Bit by bit, the story came out. Cindy told about how Vanessa had found out about the accident. Not from her father, who never heard about it, but from the garage man at Harry's. It was Vanessa, too, who'd planted the idea in Tom Gaetano's mind that Walt was insulting him behind his back.

"Why are you telling me this?" Walt asked, amazed.

Cindy shook her head in confusion. "I don't know for sure. I suppose I'm being disloyal to Vanessa. But I don't think she deserves my loyalty. And I guess I started to feel guilty. I always thought you were a nice guy. Now you're getting in trouble and it's all our fault."

"I don't think so," Walt said. "I made some of that trouble for myself. Vanessa just helped me out along the way. Come to think of it, if my head had been on straight I'd never have believed any rumor I heard from her."

"I hope you're not angry," Cindy said.

"Funny thing. This is just about the first time in weeks I *haven't* been angry," Walt answered. "But I do have some important questions to ask you."

"Me? Important?" Cindy looked confused.

"Sure. Number one: Do you like to dance? And number two: Are you busy Friday night?"

Cindy laughed. "I was expecting hard questions. Those are easy."

By the time Walt left the Burger King, he had his answers.

CHAPTER

"Here we go . . . ready or not!" Ardith Engborg announced, prepared to flip the switch connecting Walt's tape machine to the auditorium sound system.

The stands were nearly filled. A sell out crowd of home-team fans had turned out to see the Tarenton Wolves try to beat the Grove Lake Grizzlies. There was even a camera crew from the local independent TV station busily conferencing at the other end of the players' bench, waiting for the action to begin.

Out on the court, Walt and Pres had just finished arranging a long gym mat that the squad planned to use for its pre-game pep routine. After debating the matter for two days, Coach Engborg had decided to go with Walt's idea after all and do the break-dance style drill that he had worked out.

"Our practice sessions have not been exactly inspired," Ardith had announced at the pre-game meeting. "Maybe what we all need is a challenge to pull this squad together again."

Nancy Goldstein nervously fingered the red-and-white pleats of her cheerleading skirt as she waited for the music to begin. "I just hope I don't trip and fall while the camera's on me," she said.

"You'll do fine," Olivia Evans patted her on the back. "You've got the moves."

Which I don't, Mary Ellen thought nervously, as she took her place at the end of the line. Somehow, though, she felt more elated than nervous. The prospect of being on camera was enough to make her forget her reservations about this routine. It was even enough to make her forget, temporarily, that Patrick would be at the dance with Vanessa Barlow.

When Walt and Pres had returned to take their places at the head of the line, Ardith flipped the switch to start the music.

"*Baby, do the Beat Street strut . . . it's so hot. . . .*"

Its attention grabbed by the unusual music, the home crowd burst into applause. Then, as the squad took the floor, one by one, the crowd began clapping in unison.

As she waited, the last to join the line, Mary Ellen noted the others' movements admiringly. Walt, of course, was the best. His stocky body looked so unsuited to this kind of dancing that his high kicks and sinuous steps were all the more breathtaking. And when he sank to the floor for a dramatic break dance solo, the crowd burst into spontaneous applause. Even the TV crew, which had been standing around looking bored at being stuck for the evening at a mere high school game, came to life and started the cameras rolling.

Olivia, who joined Walt on the floor next, was a natural at this routine.

And Nancy, who came third, was almost as good.

Even Pres, and then Angie, did respectably. Obviously they had been getting in some extra practice.

Here goes! Mary Ellen told herself as her turn came to go out onto the floor. Giving herself up to the music, she imagined that she was the girl on the rock video, learning to dance this way for the first time. To her surprise, the make believe started to work. The pasted smile on her face started to feel real. She was enjoying herself! And for the first time, she felt natural doing the high sideways kicks and strutting steps.

The response of the crowd and the continuing interest of the TV crew, as it kept the cameras rolling, told the entire squad that the routine had caught on. About halfway through the record, a voice-over that Mary Ellen recognized as Walt's strong tenor broke into the song with a new lyric: "The *Wolves* are *so hot . . . do the Beat Street strut. . . . Beat the Grizzlies.*"

The crowd clapped wildly, then sang along.

As the tape came to an end, Mary Ellen ran to the sidelines and grabbed the megaphone, determined to keep up the pitch of excitement.

> "Hear ye . . . hear ye
> Read all about it. . . .
> We got a team.
> No doubt about it. . . .
> Clap your hands! Stamp your feet!
> The WOLVES are the team
> That can't be beat!!!"

The spirit was there. The squad was its old self again.

The action on the court, meanwhile, was not going quite so smoothly. Mary Ellen had been wondering before the game just what would happen when it came time to give individual cheers for Jimmy Hilbert's baskets. She had envisioned Olivia and Nancy practically at each other's throats vying for the honor. As it turned out, there was no opportunity for competition on that score.

After allowing a few baskets to Jimmy in the first quarter, the Grizzly defense simply double-teamed Jimmy, rendering him helpless.

"That's just what my cousin predicted," Angie muttered during an early time-out. "It's going to take more than one hot shot to beat this opponent."

"Gaetano was right about that," Walt agreed.

"Glad to hear you say so, old buddy," Pres

added. Now that his own problems were beginning to straighten out, he was finding it hard to recall exactly why he'd been so down on Walt lately. As usual, it didn't occur to him to put his change of heart into words. Pres wasn't the type to talk about his feelings more than he had to. But Walt had been around Pres long enough to recognize a peace feeler when he heard it. "See," he announced to the others, "even the great Preston Tilford III agrees with us. We must be right."

Instead of bristling at this, Pres grinned serenely. Walt was definitely back to his old self again, making wisecracks and dishing out backhanded insults.

Even Ardith Engborg couldn't help smiling with satisfaction at Walt's recovery — but only for a second or two. "We're not here to be basketball critics," she reminded everyone. "We're cheerleaders, in case you've all forgotten."

"We've got the T-E-A-M that's on the B-E-A-M. . . ." Angie shouted, leading the others into the cheer.

When the time-out ended, however, Angie really had something to shout about. Her own brother, Andrew, was being sent in to replace Jimmy Hilbert. "Andrew, Andrew, he's our man! If he can't do it, no one can!" she yelled.

Andrew's entry into the game did change the Wolves' luck. From lagging ten points behind, the team caught up to within a basket of the Grizzlies. Unfortunately, for the next three quarters it was a question of playing catch-up. Every time the Wolves narrowed the score, the Grizzlies would get a spurt of energy and pull ahead again.

Mary Ellen had never cheered so hard in her life. She cheered for Andrew. And she cheered even louder, if possible, when Hank Vreewright came into the game with his bandaged knee to make one last try for the team. The final results of the contest were in doubt right up to the last play. With just seconds to go, the Wolves had pulled to within two points of the Grizzlies once again, and Hank was loping down the floor with time for one more shot. The entire Tarenton section rose to its feet as Hank let the ball fly. Then they watched in agony as the ball lazily rolled around the hoop and dropped to one side. A moan of dismay arose spontaneously from fans and cheerleaders alike.

Oddly enough, the loss didn't seem to dim the fans' spirits. After the final buzzer sounded, the entire Tarenton section stayed on its feet while Mary Ellen and Pres led them all in the "Growl, Wolves, Growl!" cheer. Next came the Tarenton High fight song, and still no one left. Finally, after a good five or ten minutes of cheering, the fans slowly began to disperse.

"You can all be proud of yourselves tonight," Ardith told the squad as they huddled for a brief post-game meeting before going to the locker rooms. "It's easy to keep a crowd cheering for a winning team. But not every squad can keep up the energy when their team is lagging behind."

Ardith's judgment turned out to be shared by the TV news crew. That evening, on the local ten o'clock news, the clips of the game featured more than a few shots of the Tarenton cheerleading squad in action. "Tarenton basketball fans showed up in force tonight for a game that marked a new stage in the town's old rivalry with Grove Lake," was the way the sportscaster framed the story. The fact that the Grizzlies had actually won the game was mentioned only as an afterthought.

Mary Ellen, watching on a portable TV in Ardith Engborg's office, was the only member of the squad to see the news report. The rest had all gone downstairs to the cafeteria where the after-game dance was already underway.

Even Ardith was surprised that Mary Ellen was willing to miss the dance just to see the report on TV. "I'm saving this all on videotape so we can watch it tomorrow," she reminded Mary Ellen for what seemed like the hundredth time. "There's no need for you to miss the dance."

"I haven't missed anything," Mary Ellen finally said as she got up to leave after the report ended.

Before Ardith could ask for an explanation, Mary Ellen fled to the showers. She did not plan to go to the dance at all. At least that's what she'd been telling herself all day. Plenty of girls went to Friday night school dances without dates. There was no couples-only rule. But going solo to a dance was not an experience that Mary Ellen

Kirkwood ever had to face before. Nor was it one that she had any desire to go through for the first time.

Knowing that Patrick would be at the dance with Vanessa, after she'd actually broken down and suggested he take her, only made the prospect less appealing.

If she hurried, there would still be time to ask Ardith for a ride home. Mary Ellen showered and changed quickly and went over to the mirrors by the sinks to fix her hair. "Coward!" she said accusingly as she faced her own image in the mirror. "You know very well that if you don't show up at the dance, Patrick will think you stayed away because of him and Vanessa."

Of course it wasn't true.

Then, too, there was the prospect of having to explain to Ardith why she was going straight home and skipping the dance. Ardith's speech after the game had reminded everyone that the coach had no respect for quitters.

Mary Ellen studied her appearance in the mirror critically. Since the dance was being held right after the game, there was no dress code at all. Some girls would be dressed up, but others would no doubt show up in casual clothes. Still, the outfit that she had on was not what Mary Ellen Kirkwood would normally be expected to wear to a dance: tan slacks and a long-sleeved blouse that she had often worn to school, and a hand-knit vest of gold-toned wool that her sister Gemma had made and given to her for Christmas.

"Not great. Not great at all," she told herself. But it would have to do. Even if she just stayed at the dance for five minutes, it would be better than not showing up at all and letting Patrick Henley think he'd kept her away.

CHAPTER

15

For the after-game dance, the high school cafeteria had been transformed into an ice-castle fantasy. The formica tables and ugly tan chairs were gone, banished to the storerooms. The dull green walls were hidden under yards of gauzy white material. Even the old tile floor was unrecognizable, covered with silver spangles that glittered like snowflakes under the bluish spotlights.

Angie Poletti had more to be happy about than just the decorations. At the last minute, Marc had decided that he could make the time to come home for the weekend after all. As she stood near the main entrance, watching the other couples arrive, Angie felt Marc's strong hands resting lightly on her shoulders. She had all but resigned herself to attending the dance alone. Now, having Marc here with her was almost better than if it had been planned that way all along.

Angie knew why *she* was happy.

She knew why Pres was happy, too. A few minutes ago, he had come through the door with Kerry Elliott at his side, beaming proudly. No one could say Pres and Kerry were a natural couple: Pres, the golden boy, and shy Kerry, who hated the limelight. But for tonight at least, Kerry had overcome her doubts. She leaned her head against his shoulder as they danced, determined not to let all the still unanswered questions in her head drive her crazy.

It was a lot harder to figure out just what Nancy and Olivia had to be so thrilled about. By Friday afternoon, Nancy had managed to spread the news all over school that she and Jimmy Hilbert had a date for the dance that night. Angie had expected Olivia to be throwing tantrums of jealousy. Instead, the two girls had seemed to get along awfully well during tonight's game.

And in the locker room afterward, they had gone into one of the changing rooms together and come out, giggling, wearing identical dresses. Chic-looking shifts of jersey wool with raglan sleeves and wide, hip-hugging sashes. Only the colors were different. Nancy's dress was a soft shade of rose that made her dark complexion look all the more radiant; Olivia's, a vibrant purple, the kind of bright, dramatic color she seldom wore, but which made her youthful looks seem suddenly very sophisticated.

"You both look great," Angie had said admiringly.

She had not wanted to ask why both girls were wearing the same dress. Maybe it had been a coincidence, in which case the less said, the better.

But the impish looks on both their faces told her otherwise. Something was up. "So what's going on?" Angie had teased. "Are you doing an Eismar twins imitation?"

Angie hadn't gotten an answer then. Just a pair of knowing grins that said, "wait and see." But when Nancy and Olivia showed up at the door to the cafeteria still arm in arm, Angie caught on right away. She knew what was going to happen even before Jimmy Hilbert, who had been lounging by the ticket desk, happily waiting for the arrival of his date for the evening.

"Hi, Jimmy," Nancy said, ignoring the confused looks he was shooting her way. "I knew you wouldn't mind if I brought Olivia along for the evening. Since you're such good friends and all."

Without further explanation, each of the girls took one of Jimmy's arms and ushered him up to the ticket desk.

"Jimmy loves the idea of having two girls chasing him," Angie said, explaining the situation to Marc. "But I guess he didn't count on having both of them catch him at exactly the same time."

His face a picture of total resignation, Jimmy danced first with Nancy, then with Olivia, then with Nancy again.

By the end of the set, though, he was alone. While he was taking his turn with Olivia, Michael calmly strode onto the floor and cut in. Nancy, meanwhile, had begun dancing with Andrew Poletti.

Jimmy stood in the middle of the floor for a minute or two, looking bewildered. Then he slunk off in the direction of the refreshments.

Angie and Marc, who were taking a break themselves, noticed Jimmy's fate. "I almost feel sorry for him," Angie said. "Or I would if the whole thing weren't so funny."

"Vanessa won't like this," a voice from behind them predicted. "She was counting on Nancy and Olivia to cancel each other out by making a scene. Then she would swoop down and steal him from both of them. Somehow, though, I don't think this was the kind of scene she had in mind."

Angie turned around. The voice belonged to Cindy Hartman, who was looking unusually pretty in a pale blue blouse and black, ankle-length slacks. And with her was Walt.

"You'll be happy to know I'm not flunking English after all," Walt announced. "Thanks to Cindy here."

Walt explained that he had turned in the first installment of his journal, and would be catching up by doing extra writing after school for the next two weeks. "Your cousin is actually a pretty nice guy after all," Walt conceded to Angie. "I'm sorry I ever doubted it. It was my fault, but my feud with Mr. Gaetano did get a little boost from

Vanessa. It took Cindy here to remind me of who my friends were."

Angie looked at Cindy questioningly. "But aren't you —"

"Vanessa's shadow?" Cindy suggested, finishing Angie's thought for her. "I was, but no more. I've resigned."

"Speak of the devil. . . ." Marc's deep baritone voice boomed out louder than he had intended. All eyes turned toward the door.

Vanessa had arrived. She was wearing a full-skirted red dress with a plunging neckline and ankle strap shoes. At her side was Patrick Henley. Judging from the way Vanessa posed in the doorway, Patrick was no more than just another part of her get-up for the evening. And not the most important part, at that.

When Vanessa accepted Patrick's invitation to the dance, she had never intended to stick with him all evening. And certainly she didn't plan to be taken home in the Henley Trash pickup truck. Her original plans had called for her to dance with Patrick the first hour or so. Just long enough to set up her move on Jimmy Hilbert.

Vanessa hadn't known earlier in the week who would end up being Jimmy's date for the dance — Nancy or Olivia. But she had bet that either girl would be driving Jimmy crazy with jealous questions about the other. Maybe they'd even end up quarreling. And that would be her golden opportunity.

Scanning the room from the doorway, Vanessa

realized that part of her plan hadn't worked out. Mary Ellen was nowhere in sight. So her entrance on Patrick's arm had been at least partly wasted.

On the other hand, Jimmy was standing all alone over by the punch bowl.

Vanessa saw no reason to hang around with Patrick a minute longer. "See you later," she said, dismissing Patrick without regret. And she made a beeline across the floor in Jimmy's direction.

Marc, Angie, Walt, and Cindy all watched with interest the look of rising panic on Jimmy's face. When Vanessa was five feet away, he suddenly turned around and bolted out the door.

"Gee," Angie said, "what got into him? I thought he and Vanessa would make the perfect couple."

"Some other time, maybe," Marc mused. "If you ask me, Jimmy has had too much girl trouble for one day. He just wasn't ready to take on Vanessa, too."

Marc put his arm around Angie's shoulder and steered her back out onto the dance floor. "Let's forget about Vanessa for now. We're together. That's what counts."

"Right you are," Angie agreed. And she closed her eyes and rested her head on Marc's shoulder. For the rest of the evening, being with Marc was enough to put her on top of the world.

At the moment, togetherness was the last thing on Mary Ellen's mind.

She had purposely waited out in the hall until

a slow dance started, hoping to time her solo entrance so that it attracted the minimum attention. At the moment when the lights were at their dimmest, she judged that her chance had come. Straightening her spine and squaring her shoulders, she stepped through the door.

"Melon!"

The sound of the nickname she hated, booming out in Patrick's idea of a normal conversational voice, made her want to cringe. But it was too late. Patrick had spotted her entrance immediately and was already at her side.

"Where's Vanessa?" Mary Ellen asked coldly, forgetting for a second that she was not supposed to care.

"I got dumped," Patrick said cheerfully. "I should have known that Vanessa had an ulterior motive for coming with me. I guess I just got carried away, thinking she was mesmerized by my great body. Anyway, forget Vanessa. Let's dance."

Mary Ellen yearned to be in his arms. But her feelings were in a turmoil. I'm the one who's mesmerized, she thought. "Why should I dance with you," she said aloud, "after you turned me down for another girl?"

Patrick shrugged. "No reason. Unless it's because you want to. You know I only came with her to make you jealous."

Mary Ellen watched in confusion as Patrick began to walk away from her. The fact was, she did want to. There was no use pretending otherwise.

"Hey, wait a minute!" she said, calling him back. "Don't tell me you're going to give up so easily."

"What do you think?" Patrick asked. And without another word, he swept her into his arms and out onto the dance floor. Neither of them spoke again for as long as the song lasted. For two people who could barely have a conversation without getting into an argument, they danced smoothly together, as if they belonged in each other's arms. Mary Ellen's blonde head next to Patrick's dark one made a handsome contrast.

As the last strains of the music died away, Patrick cupped Mary Ellen's face in his big, work-hardened hands. "You really are an impossible girl to figure out," he said. "Does this mean you're going to stop fighting your feelings for me? Is tonight a beginning for us? Or is this only a temporary truce?"

For one heart-twisting moment, Mary Ellen felt tempted to give Patrick the answer he wanted to hear. She opened her mouth to speak, only to see him shake his head in warning. "Forget it," he said. "I guess I'm not ready for an honest answer to that one. I'd rather just enjoy being with you right now."

The music started up again, another slow song. Mary Ellen rested her head dreamily against Patrick's muscular shoulder. For the moment, being close to Patrick felt completely right. She tried her best to pretend that the feeling would last forever. But she knew herself too well. To-morrow all her old yearnings for a different kind of life would start again. But just for tonight, Patrick's arms around her and his lips against her cheek were all she wanted.

If Nancy thinks Jimmy was trouble, wait until she meets Ben! Read Cheerleaders #5, ALL THE WAY.

A new book each month!

The cheerleaders of Tarenton High have it all—love, prestige, triumph, popularity, and excitement! Keep up with the dynamic lives of the Cheerleaders™ month after month as the drama continues...

Watch for these new titles!

Trying Out
by Caroline B. Cooney
(*January*)

There are only four coveted positions open this year on Tarenton High's prestigious cheerleading squad. Sixty girls are trying out...the competition is intense...and the tensions are mounting high!

Getting Even
by Christopher Pike
(*February*)

Vanessa is out for revenge. Her weapon? Blackmail! Can she get her rival for homecoming queen kicked off the cheerleading squad...for good?

Rumors
by Caroline B. Cooney
(*March*)

Mary Ellen never has any money...so how come she suddenly has the most beautiful wardrobe at Tarenton High? And why is it that Angie, who's always struggled to keep her C-average, is suddenly making the honor roll? And just what is going on between Angie and Pres?

All the Way
by Caroline B. Cooney
(*May*)

Nancy finds new love with the captain of the basketball team...Tarenton's arch rival, that is! As the race between the two schools comes down to the wire, Nancy finds herself torn. Can she remain loyal to Tarenton High?

Splitting
by Jennifer Sarasin
(*June*)

Pres has had it! He wants out of his parents' home—even if it means getting kicked off the squad. Thanks to Vanessa, he just might be...

Everything you've always wanted...and more!

from 📚 Scholastic Inc. $2.25 each

Books chosen with you in mind from

—Pass the word.

Living...loving...growing.
That's what **POINT** books are all about!
They're books you'll love reading and
will want to tell your friends about.

Don't miss these other exciting **Point** titles!

NEW POINT TITLES! $2.25 each

☐ QI 33306-2 **The Karate Kid** B.B. Hiller
☐ QI 31987-6 **When We First Met** Norma Fox Mazer
☐ QI 32512-4 **Just the Two of Us** Hila Colman
☐ QI 32338-5 **If This Is Love, I'll Take Spaghetti** Ellen Conford
☐ QI 32728-3 **Hello...Wrong Number** Marilyn Sachs
☐ QI 33216-3 **Love Always, Blue** Mary Pope Osborne
☐ QI 33116-7 **The Ghosts of Departure Point** Eve Bunting
☐ QI 33195-7 **How Do You Lose Those Ninth Grade Blues?** Barthe DeClements
☐ QI 33550-2 **Charles In Charge** Elizabeth Faucher
☐ QI 32306-7 **Take It Easy** Steven Kroll
☐ QI 33409-3 **Slumber Party** Christopher Pike

Scholastic Inc.
P.O. Box 7502, 2932 East McCarty Street, Jefferson City, MO 65102

Please send me the books I have checked above. I am enclosing
$_____ (please add $1.00 to cover shipping and handling). Send
check or money order—no cash or C.O.D.'s please.

Name_____

Address_____

City_____ State/Zip_____

POI851   Please allow four to six weeks for delivery.

Books Ablaze with Historical Romance...

SUNFIRE™

Meet these fascinating young women who dared to be different during the most exciting and turbulent times in America! Sunfire ... thrilling novels of adventure and romance.